# Freed from MOROCCO

## LESLIE HACHTEL

# Also Available from Leslie Hachtel

**Historical**
The Defiant Bride
Captain's Captive
Hannah's War

**Romantic Suspense**
Texas Summer
Payback
Once Upon a Tablecloth

**The Dance Series**
The Dream Dancer
Emma's Dance
The Jester's Dance
A Dance in Time

**The Morocco Series**
Bound to Morocco
Tied to Morocco

**Anthology**
Grave Importance

# Table of Contents

## Dedication

To all my readers, who go with me on these fabulous adventures. I love having your company!

# Acknowledgments

To the amazing Jenn Bray-Weber whose editing talent always makes the work better.
To Jena Brignola whose artistic talent brings my vision to life.
To Judi Fennell—I couldn't do it without you!
Thank you all!!!!

# Chapter One

*Spring, 1717*

Olivia Kincaid could barely breathe. Awakening in the stifling confines of an airless space, her head was beating a painful rhythm that reverberated into the rest of her aching body. Her jaw pulsated and her teeth throbbed. The heavy smell of old wood and moldy air irritated her nostrils and her mouth felt as though it had been dragged through a desert. She was terribly thirsty. And what was that incessant creaking noise? She blinked and her eyes were as dry as sand, her vision blurred. Tentatively, she sat up and gazed around.

Her hands burned at the wrists, as did the skin above her ankles. She had obviously been bound at some point, as evidenced by the red welts where the restraints had dug into her flesh. She rubbed the offended areas as she scanned the small space. *Oh, dear God.* She squeezed her eyes shut, forcing the memories to gather. All the horror came flooding back, slamming into her with an appalling rush. And with the clarity came a tightness in her chest, her limbs turning to liquid.

She had been home in her bed and had just drifted off to sleep when she heard a shuffling from the corner. The room was very dark, and she squinted to see a man now standing above her. Thinking it was Tristan not wishing to draw attention to a clandestine tryst, her heart had beat faster. Would he dare sneak into her room? The excited anticipation had lasted only the barest of seconds. A hand pressed down upon her mouth, stifling sound and breath. This was not Tristan! He would never be so rough and whoever was in her bedchamber accosting her reeked of sour sweat and onions. She had realized the man had pinned her in place with the sheet and she had been unable to move her arms. Blood had pounded in her head, her heart beating a staccato of terror mixed with rage. Fury had shoved its way to the fore. She had kicked out and bucked, but whoever the man was, he had been too strong. Nabil? The man had been a constant torment to her family. He had even threatened her life years ago. He had escaped from prison, but would he dare breach the walls of Kincaid Manor? The possibility had given her new strength and she had managed to release one of her arms. She had curved her hand into a claw and connected with the flesh of his cheek. She dug in and knew she had drawn blood. He had grunted, before a blow to her jaw had her seeing stars. Still she had fought like a wildcat, scratching and striking out. A second blow and she had seen nothing more. Until now.

Fear enveloped her as she knew now, without doubt, where she was being taken. She had heard the stories so many times from her sister, Catherine, and her sister-in-law, Shera. They had described this in detail from their time in captivity on a vessel. The small, dark chamber, the walls with chains hanging from them. Even the coarse, lumpy mattresses which offered no comfort or buffer from the hard floor.

The rhythmic rocking irrevocably confirmed her dreaded conclusion. She was now certain that, like Catherine and Shera, she, too, had been kidnapped and was on a ship that would be headed for Morocco. Nabil had done this. The man who cared for naught but revenge and improving his position with his sultan. Olivia would be given to Sultan Ismail Moulay as a means of advancing Nabil's position. She would become a slave in the sultan's harem. But unlike when Catherine and Shera had been taken, this time Moulay had a vendetta. He believed Olivia's family had stolen much from him and he would not rest until he exacted retribution. Terror scraped her insides raw. Trembling shook her and sobs tore from her chest.

From the swaying of the vessel, she guessed they had not raised the anchor as yet. Perhaps she could make her way out of here before they sailed. She eased herself to standing and made her way to the door. Defeat weakened her resolve when she noted there was no knob. She pushed against the portal, but it held tight. She was locked in and she knew crying out would be useless. She had to be in the bowels of the ship, so no one would hear her.

She sank back onto a mattress and tears made more trails down her cheeks. Finally exhausted from weeping, she inhaled and forced herself to examine her situation. A tiny light of hope pierced the anxiety. Both Shera and Catherine had escaped and found their way home. Olivia, too, could get away. It was possible. It had to be. Her heart slowed its thudding against her ribs. But then, the dark cloud descended. Shera had been kidnapped by Olivia's brother, John, who actually saved her. And Catherine had been aided by John's friend Bekir, who now lived in England. But Olivia had no one to offer her aid here. She was alone. If one of her family members came for her, they would immediately be recognized and, no doubt, executed. And Bekir was with Shera's maid, Poppy, happily married and settled back home.

3

Another thought tightened her throat and twisted her stomach. What had happened to her family? What of Tristan? When she was taken, had they been attacked, as well? Nabil would have had others with him. She and Tristan had been ambushed where they met in the woods a few days earlier and Tristan had been badly beaten. Could he even defend himself in his condition now? Were any of her family harmed or even…alive?

She had been angry with her family for trying to keep her from Tristan, the man she loved. Their disapproval was unreasonable. His half-brother had proven to be a villain, but Tristan was not like his sibling. So, would they all think she had run away? She immediately dismissed that thought, realizing she wasn't thinking clearly. Tristan was still staying at her home, recovering from that attack by…surely the men that now held her captive. So Tristan should still be there, and they would all certainly know she was kidnapped by Nabil's men, would they not? *Please God, let them all be safe.* Her breath came fast, too fast, and dizziness made the room spin. She must remain calm. Her family would have defended themselves against the evildoers. And they would not allow her to languish as Moulay's captive. There was a way out of this. She just had to decide what to do. She forced any negative thoughts away. She repeated the positive thoughts in her head: her family would figure out what had happened to her, and they would not abandon her to this terrible fate.

\*\*\*

The crack of the bedchamber door as it slammed against the wall reverberated and the door nearly broke off its hinges. Shaken from the depths of his rest, Tristan

Bathurst sat straight up, his heart pounding with anticipation and confusion. He immediately regretted the quick reaction. Pain radiated down his sides, but he quelled the urge to complain. Something was very wrong.

"Tristan. Wake up!" John Kincaid burst inside, his demanding tone confirming something was amiss. "Is Olivia here with you? Are you hiding her?"

Tristan was shocked at the accusation. Did his host think him so without principle that he would seduce an innocent maiden to his bed in her family's home? That he would abuse their hospitality in such a dishonorable way?

He vibrated with rage from the insult. "I would never disgrace you or Olivia with such an act. I am a gentleman." He nodded hard to emphasize his words.

"Olivia is missing. Have you seen her?" This time John's voice had a plaintive tone.

Tristan jumped from the bed and grabbed a robe. He was still sore from the beating he had just recently sustained. Olivia's family had not approved of him, so he and Olivia had continued to meet in secret. They had no sooner reunited in the woods when they had been set upon by three men. Taken completely unawares, Olivia had thankfully escaped unharmed. It still shamed him that he had not been the one to protect her. Clearly, the miscreants did not intend to hurt her. Tristan was their target and he had been badly injured. His ribs still screamed, and every muscle was angry. Sleep had been elusive, so the doctor had given him a sleeping potion and he had been deeply asleep until a moment ago. But now his physical discomfort was forgotten.

"Have you checked her room?" He realized the folly of his question as soon as he asked it. John's look of disdain confirmed his irritation. "I'm sorry. Of course you did. But where could she have gone?" His chest tightened

5

at the idea that Olivia might be in danger. Sheer terror for her safety suffused him with dread. If anything happened to her, he would kill the person who so much as laid a hand on her. He vowed he would not rest until she was safely home. He would not fail her again.

But John had already left the room and was rushing down the corridor. Tristan was on his heels as they both tore down the stairs. The rest of the family was clustered together in the foyer. Lady Philippa, Olivia's mother, was openly weeping. Shera clung to her children, little Malcolm and tiny Edwina, while Catherine was huddled against her husband, Tazim. The earl, Olivia's father, paced furiously, his hands clasped behind his back.

All looked to John as he stomped down the last step. "She is gone. Tristan has not seen her." John said this with such finality, it was as if he had just declared her dead. For that is what they all feared. If what they imagined had happened, her life was truly at risk.

"She's just a child," Philippa moaned.

While seven and ten, Olivia was the youngest daughter. But Tristan saw Olivia not as a child but a budding woman.

"She is not so young and you must remember she is strong," John responded, patting his mother's shoulder.

Catherine moved to her mother and enfolded her in her arms. "I agree with John. And we know where she has gone, and we will get her back. Shera and I found our way home. Olivia will come home, too." But none of them seemed too convinced. *Come home?* Now Tristan was completely confused.

The earl stepped forward. "Yes, we know who took her and why," he ground out. "Nabil is dead, but I am certain his cohorts are acting on orders from the sultan himself."

6

"Wait, what?" Tristan was completely confused. "What has happened? Where is Olivia? And who is Nabil?"

John explained that Nabil was an evil man who was loyal only to himself and his sultan. He had managed to trap Catherine into marriage after arranging for her true love and now husband, Tazim, to be arrested. Catherine had escaped Nabil, but he had followed her to England. He had been sent to the gaol, but managed to find his way out.

Tazim had freed himself from prison and, after locating some of the sultan's stolen treasure, had come to England to find Catherine, as well.

John went on to recount how Nabil and his men had conspired to kill John and Tazim and take Catherine and her nephew, Malcolm, back to Morocco. The Kincaids had been delighted in their defeat of this terrible plot just hours ago, until they learned a few moments ago that Olivia was gone.

Every fiber of Tristan's being ached with the knowledge. It was as if his heart had been torn from his chest. He wanted to find her, bring her back, but he had no idea what to do. He was completely at a loss. He would go to the ends of the earth to save her.

"We must go now and find her. Why do we dawdle when we should be taking action?" Tristan demanded.

John placed a placating hand on Tristan's forearm. "We must not be hasty. It could be dangerous. We need to prepare a plan and then act on it."

Tristan knew John spoke the truth, but his immediate desire was to do something. Instead, he forced himself to calm down and listen to the earl.

"Again, we know where they will take her. That is in our favor," the earl continued. He was trying to sound logical, but there was an unmistakable tremor in his voice. "What we need is a strategy. So, we must remain clear-headed enough so we can save her." This last was directed at Tristan.

Tristan took a moment to understand all that had occurred while he slept. Shame washed through him. "Why did no one call me. I could have helped."

"There was no time," John assured him. "And it was actually Catherine who saved the day."

Tazim, Catherine's husband, pulled her close and kissed her on the mouth. Her arms went around his waist.

"It wasn't as if I did it alone," she said, rolling her eyes.

"She stabbed Nabil with a hairpin," Tazim said with obvious pride, "and gave us the opening we needed to take down the others." Tristan knew Olivia had the same kind of courage.

Stephen, Tazim's valet and trusted friend, strode into the door. "If Olivia is to be loaded onto a ship, there is a chance it has not sailed. The scum who came with Nabil may not know he has been killed. They might delay in hopes he will appear with Lady Catherine and young Malcolm. I will ride to the docks and possibly intercede before they raise the anchor," he declared.

"Even in death, the man haunts us," John sneered.

"I will go with you," Tazim said, joining Stephen. A few moments later, the thundering of horses' hooves could be heard in the foyer.

Tristan rocked back on his heels and inhaled slowly. Again, he had failed the love of his life. Fury raced through his blood, his heart pumping hard with his frustration. He must think rationally. Whatever it took, no matter what the cost, he was going to get his beloved Olivia back home safely. He would never disappoint her again. Never! Plans flitted in and out of his thoughts. He tamped down the bitter bile of dissatisfaction with determination. There had to be a way and he would find it.

***

Scuffling and the piercing sound of women shrieking had Olivia sitting up straighter. The cabin door flung open and two young women were thrust into the room. She caught a glimpse of the man who had shoved them forward. His Moroccan garb confirmed what she already knew of her captors. Olivia forced back a sob as the first woman stumbled into the room and the second one fell over her in a jumble of arms and legs. They lay there unmoving for a moment, and then their outraged protests filled the air. The door slammed and the lock struck home. Olivia knew a small thrill of relief at seeing the others and immediately felt guilty. She would not have to suffer this voyage alone and perhaps these two could help in planning an escape. But she was sad that they must share her fate. However, their cacophony of distress was not helping her headache.

The women, who appeared to be about her own age, slowly untangled themselves as best they could manage. They stood, clasped their hands together, and touched foreheads. Then, looking about, they realized they were not alone. Together, they turned to Olivia, as if seeking answers. Olivia closed her eyes and shook her head in sympathy.

"Who are you," one of the women asked, though it was more of a demand.

"I am a prisoner, too," she replied softly.

"Prisoners. But that is not possible," declared the other woman. "Is it?"

Their loud shrieks, followed by a shrill sobbing,

fairly shook the walls. Olivia inhaled, and waited for the storm to pass. Finally, the noise diminished to sniffling.

"What is happening?" asked one, her voice wavering with anxiety. "Why, we have only just arrived back from France and we were to be met by a coach. Why have we been forced onto this ship? And why do you say we are captive here. And where are we going?"

"We are going on an adventure." Olivia was trying for bravado but couldn't maintain it. Tears coursed down her cheeks.

"Do you know who is responsible and where they are taking us?" The second girl's voice trembled, too, with her apprehension. "And why? And who would dare do this to us? Do they not know who we are?"

"I wish to go home," whined the first girl. "The voyage home was sufficiently unsatisfactory. I have no desire to spend more time on the water." She scowled at Olivia. "Call someone," she demanded.

Olivia took a deep breath. She wanted to sound composed, as expressing her own fears would not help this situation. "My name is Olivia Kincaid. And to answer one of your questions, we are all now captive and sailing to Morocco."

"Morocco," one screeched. "That uncivilized land? I have no desire to go there. I want off this ship." She jumped up and down several times, then smoothed her skirts. "Do you hear me?" she screamed. "I want off this ship!" She glared at Olivia. "Just look at my dress! Can you not see what they have done to my new gown?" She sobbed in outrage.

"Who are you?" Olivia asked quietly, hoping to change the subject and perhaps calm the woman.

Peering down her nose, she responded haughtily. "I

am Lady Amelia Caswell, and this is my older sister, Lady Charlotte. We cannot abide this treatment. I must protest, I tell you." She stuck her chin in the air to emphasize her displeasure, as if Olivia could intercede for them.

Olivia nearly burst out laughing at the ludicrous arrogance of the statement but managed to control her mirth. The two looked very much alike, with pale blond hair and light eyes. Their cheeks had never been exposed to sunlight and they reflected the protected lives they had led—until today, that is. Their gowns were expensive, but now both were dirty and torn. These poor girls had no idea what or who they were dealing with. And they needed to learn in a hurry, lest they give offense to the wrong person. Obviously, they had been carefully raised among the gentry, so Olivia would need to enlighten them gently.

"Listen to me carefully as, unfortunately, I know whereof I speak." Olivia crossed her hands over her heart and sucked in a deep breath. The two tilted their heads in unison and looked at her with open mouths, but they said nothing.

"As I mentioned before, I am quite certain we have been kidnapped and are being taken to Morocco, to the land of Sultan Ismail Moulay." She managed to keep her tone very matter of fact.

Charlotte's face lit up and she eased herself down onto a mattress. Amelia plopped down beside her sister, a spark of interest in her expression. "A sultan?" Charlotte said, smiling excitedly. "Well, he will certainly recognize our nobility and welcome us. Our father is a viscount. Another ruler will surely respect this and will then entertain us at his…does a sultan live in a castle?" Her tone was that of a young child.

She looked to her sister, who shrugged. "But only until he books us passage home," Amelia stated. "It will be like a holiday." Charlotte nodded her agreement.

Olivia found their naiveté ridiculous. "You, I mean we, will not be experiencing luxurious accommodations. And there will be no passage back home. We will be sent to live with other women in a harem and we will be at the sultan's pleasure, to do with as he pleases." She whispered the last part. Voicing it made it too real.

"Oh, do not be so silly." Amelia waved her left wrist forward in dismissal. "This is simply a terrible mistake." With that, she stood up again and nearly lost her footing when the ship rocked. She righted herself and stomped to the door and proceeded to hit it with her fists. "Someone, anyone. I need to speak with whoever is in charge here," she demanded. When no one responded, she commenced banging again.

"Please stop," Olivia said quietly. "Your pounding will only serve to deafen us." She closed her eyes and prayed for patience.

Amelia stuck out her tongue at Olivia, but ceased her noise. She trudged over to another mattress and flopped back down, tears of obvious frustration coursing down her cheeks. "Not even a proper bed," she whimpered. "Do these savages have no idea who they are dealing with?"

A loud groaning and creaking shook the room and Olivia knew they were now underway. If she hadn't thought as much before, now Olivia was convinced her voyage to Morocco would not be as pleasant as Shera's had been. Olivia's brother, John, had been in charge then and he and Shera had fallen in love. But, initially, Shera must have been terrified. As Catherine had been. Just as Olivia was now. Her two companions were not helping ease her tension. In fact, there were already causing complications. "Please. I am trying to help you. You need to listen and follow my instructions."

Amelia spun on her. "Who are you to tell us what to

do? And how is it you know so much about everything?" she snarled.

"Yes," her sister echoed, narrowing her eyes. "How is that? Are you in it with the kidnappers?" Poison oozed in her tone. "You have the dark hair and eyes of someone *not* born in England." She lifted a shoulder. "How do we know you are not merely going back to your home country?" Amelia nodded.

Olivia managed to control her irritation. "Do I appear as if I am a kidnapper? Or am I occupying the same space as you two?" She shook her head in frustration. "And do I speak as one from another country?"

"You did not answer our question," Charlotte persisted. "And how would we know you are not here as a spy." She looked to Amelia for confirmation and her sister stuck out her lower lip and nodded again in affirmation.

Olivia heaved a sigh. "I know so much because both my sister and my sister-in-law suffered the same fate as we do now."

Amelia tilted her head and scoffed. "Well, that is not possible."

"It *is* possible since it truly happened." Olivia was defensive now. She disliked the insinuation she was a liar. "They both managed to escape, but not without suffering. And, if you two wish to return home in your lifetime, I suggest you listen to what I tell you."

"Why would we listen to anything you have to tell us? After all, we are nobility." Amelia sneered.

Olivia's smile slowly lifted her lips. "As am I. Did I not mention that I, too, carry a title?"

Charlotte gasped and her mouth dropped open as realization dawned. "Kincaid, as in the earl?"

"Yes," Olivia affirmed. "As in the earl. I am his daughter."

13

"She outranks us," Charlotte whispered, dropping her head in a mock bow. Amelia reluctantly followed suit.

"All right, all right," Amelia said, dismissively. She slumped onto one of the mattresses covering the floor and pouted. "What do we need to do to go home?"

\*\*\*

Tazim and Stephen trudged through the front door, their faces betraying their failure. "Sailed. We missed them by an hour," Tazim fumed. "There were two ships. One still sits in the harbor. We can only guess this was the one waiting for Catherine and Nabil. It is manned by mercenary sailors who were told only that they should wait until someone arrives to give them instruction."

"Did they see Olivia taken aboard the other vessel?" Tristan asked. His thoughts twisted in a whirlwind. Olivia must be so frightened. He must do something. Perhaps if they hurried, they could still catch up to the ship.

"One of them said he saw a group board, but it was too dark to see who was among them," Stephen responded, his voice tight.

"This is like dealing with the Hydra of Greek mythology. Cut off a head and two more appear in its place." John paced the sitting room, frustration coming off him in waves. "Will we never be free of Morocco?" He hesitated, his finger tapping his lips. "I can consign a ship with a loyal crew. I have connections and a captain we can trust. It will only take a few days. Then, we can reach Moroccan shores with men we can count on."

Tristan's insides were churning, but he wished to appear reasonable. This family had to allow him to help rescue Olivia and they needed to believe he was up to the task.

"And then what?" Tazim asked. "We would all be identified and stopped. This is what they are expecting. What they are, no doubt, hoping for. We must figure a way to gain the advantage."

Tristan solemnly nodded. "That is true. They would recognize all of you. But they might not recognize an English ambassador. And how would it be if that ambassador had something to offer that might open negotiations with the sultan?"

"Something to offer," John echoed. "What do you suggest?"

"I was just wondering. What if said ambassador had managed to confiscate Moulay's treasure." He knew he was moving onto dangerous ground, but Olivia's fate was in the balance.

Tazim raised an eyebrow. "And what do you know of the sultan's treasure?"

"Olivia told me. She was very excited to relate the tale. She thought it was the stuff of which legends are made."

Tazim did not react to the compliment. His thoughts were clearly elsewhere. "You know, that idea has some possibilities." He blew out a breath. "But would that be enough to sway Moulay? After all, he believes the treasure to belong to him, so we would only be returning his own property."

"What if we offered him more?" Tristan suggested.

No one spoke, waiting expectantly for his plan. A plan he wasn't even certain would work. But it was all he had at the moment.

"What do you think he would say to improving trade relations with England?"

The earl shook his head. "The king would never

agree to that. Olivia's life is everything to us, but there would certainly be political repercussions. We cannot make such decisions without the approval of our monarch and to gain an audience and petition him would take days, or weeks."

Tristan grinned and shrugged. "Who says he has to know?" He was willing to take the risk if it would save Olivia.

Realization dawned and the earl frowned. "I suppose there would be no way for the king to have knowledge of this. But we must be very clever."

Tazim turned pointedly to Stephen. "And I know just the man who can come up with an appropriate disguise." Stephen nodded in acquiescence. Tazim then smiled at Tristan and gave a mock bow. "Mr. Ambassador."

It was Stephen who had helped disguise Tazim after he made his way to England to find Catherine. Of course, at the time, Tazim's motive was revenge, for he thought she had betrayed him and sentenced him to a miserable life in prison. When he found out that was not the case, his anger turned to shame, and he then had to prove his love for her.

Tristan recalled the tale of Catherine and Tazim's ordeal to find each other again. It was noble and he would do whatever it took to prove his love for Olivia.

Tristan's brow creased. "The treasure is not mine to offer. If we go with my strategy, it would mean you must give up your wealth, Tazim."

"Coin means naught when it comes to saving Olivia. I will gladly relinquish it. It was never mine in the first place." He had found the stolen jewels after he escaped from that wrongful imprisonment. His cellmate had told him of the location before he succumbed to death, and Tazim had left Morocco a rich man.

16

Catherine threw her arms around Tazim's waist, her love for him shining in her eyes.

"We will not let you starve." She smiled at her husband, who patted her hand.

"I was not concerned." He kissed her forehead.

John addressed the valet. "Stephen, would you go back to the docks and see about securing passage to Morocco on that ship for the English ambassador? Catherine, he will need a letter of introduction from the court."

She grinned. "And, of course, you remember calligraphy is one of my talents."

"I am your brother. I know everything." There were several snickers at this.

"And I will teach you some of the language," Tazim said to Tristan. "I can only hope you are a quick study, since we haven't much time."

"You must be aware you are putting your life in jeopardy, Tristan," John informed him quietly. "If you are discovered or the sultan happens to don a yellow or red cloak when you are in his presence, you will not only fail my sister, you will die in the attempt."

Tristan straightened his spine. "If you are not already aware," he said, echoing John's sentiment, "I am in love with Olivia. My life means naught without her. I never dreamed of actually falling in love, but it has happened, and I would risk all to save her." He dropped his chin. "When the men set upon me in the woods, I was ill-prepared and did not protect Olivia the way I should have. And tonight, she was taken, and I was again not there to save her. I have much to make up for and I will not disappoint her again."

"Bravely spoken," said John, patting Tristan on the shoulder. "Let us hope that strength does not fail you."

Tristan narrowed his eyes. Was that meant as a slight? "Think you because I grew up in a noble household that I am a weakling? That I cannot bravely face adversity? Or that I am anything like my half-brother?"

Tazim took a step toward him. "No, Tristan, he does not think that at all. It is just—well, Morocco is a different world and some of the things that happen there are beyond your imagination." His tone was placating, and Tristan acknowledged it as such, then lifted his chin.

"All the more reason to rescue Olivia as quickly as possible. Do you not agree?"

*** 

The first morning on the ship, servants arrived with a pile of garments for the women, which they unceremoniously dumped in a corner before retreating. Amelia was the first to examine the clothing, holding up pants and what appeared to be an embroidered vest.

"Where are the corsets?" she demanded. Her voice was unpleasantly loud in the small space.

"They do not wear them," Olivia stated flatly.

"How unladylike," Charlotte sneered. "These people are savages, just as I said. Perhaps we can teach them some manners."

Olivia ignored her and sorted through the available outfits. She selected a pair of loose, silky pants, a white shirt, a scarf artfully sewn with flowers and exotic birds embroidered into the fabric, and a sleeveless over-vest. All the garments were woven with beautiful, bright colors and skillfully crafted. Olivia turned her back to the others and shrugged out of her dress and undergarments, then slipped on the soft clothes. She wrapped the scarf around her waist to hold up the pants and was delighted at how comfortable the attire felt.

She turned back and the sisters glared at her as if she had grown another head.

"You look like a man," Charlotte derided her. "And an uncivilized one at that."

Amelia immediately agreed with a nod of her head. Olivia just shrugged.

"My gown is dirty and torn and I, for one, appreciate clean clothes. This is what is offered. Take it or not." Her patience was worn to a nub.

"Well, I, for one…" Amelia sneered, "will maintain myself as a lady."

Time dragged as though a demon pinned it down by the coattails. Men would arrive each morning with fruits, flatbreads and tea. The three would partake of the meal, Olivia silent amid the grousing of the sisters.

In the afternoon, guards would re-appear, cover the women's faces with veils, and lead them up to the deck. The first time they came to the door to escort the women above deck, Charlotte had started to scream. Both the guards and Olivia looked at her as if she had completely lost her mind. Then Amelia joined in and the combination of the two screeching made Olivia's ears feel like they were bleeding. The guards ducked their heads to ease the burden of the racket.

"Why are you shouting about?" Olivia yelled over the terrible din.

"They are going to hurt us." Charlotte squealed.

Olivia blew out a frustrated breath. "They are taking us up on deck to get some air." She tried not to sound as if she were addressing an idiot.

Both women calmed after a moment. "How do you

know?" Amelia whispered, as if they could not be overheard.

"Because, I told you, both my sister and sister-in-law have been in our position." Exasperation edged out through her clenched teeth.

"But what will they do to us?" Charlotte demanded.

"Not a thing but guard you and watch to see you do not fall overboard. They will not harm you. You are now considered a possession of the sultan and it would mean their lives if they laid a single finger on your person."

Amelia lifted her chin. "I am no one's possession," she huffed.

Olivia shook her head. "Have it your way. It matters not. Just know you are safe on this ship."

"How can you say that? We are here against our will." This from Charlotte.

"Would you like to take a walk in some fresh air, and get out of this stuffy cabin or not?" Olivia was truly tiring of this discourse.

Both women acquiesced after a moment and allowed veils to be placed on their faces.

Olivia savored the times when they were allowed up on deck to breathe the fresh sea breezes. The sunlight shimmered on the water, which became a more vibrant blue the further south they traveled. The ocean on the right side of the vessel stretched forever to the horizon and Olivia occupied her thoughts with the life that lived beneath the surface. All manner of creatures, both real and mythical, seeking their destinies. Coming and going as the spirit moved them.

Tamping down the jealousy of that freedom, she looked to the left. Too far to shore. She tried to guess if it was Spain or Portugal, but it mattered little. These places were not the final destination. An errant thought of diving into the water and swimming to safety was quickly dismissed. She was not a strong swimmer and the distance was too great. She would drown in the attempt, if one of the sea creatures she had read about did not devour her. But then, would that be more terrible than her fate in Morocco? Yes, she decided. As long as she drew breath, there was a chance she could find her way home.

During these respites, Olivia made it a point to stretch her muscles and move about as much as possible in the limited space. The other two women would look down their noses in obvious disgust, leaning against the railing and squinting and ducking their faces away from the bright sunlight. But being in the outdoors and even this meager exercise made Olivia feel better.

The nights were the most difficult. When the sisters finally settled to sleep and it was blessedly quiet, Olivia's thoughts drifted to her home and her family. There was a huge, empty space in her chest that throbbed with loneliness. She missed Tristan most of all. She had fallen deeply in love with him the moment she set eyes on him and she knew he had felt the same. He was kind and gentle and so handsome. He made her laugh. He was the man she had conjured up as a husband when she was but a little girl spinning her imaginings. Now, being here without him was like losing a part of herself. Of course, she missed her family, too, but it was not the same.

She and Tristan had talked of their lives together as soon as they could wed, of the children they would have. They had pressed their lips together and Olivia had been transported to a magic land where nothing mattered but the sensations coursing through her body. Now, it all seemed like a story she had made up, one that would never have the chance to end happily. She prayed that they all, at least, were safe. But she knew they would not rest until she was back home with them and free from the control of the demon who ruled even on this ship. Believing her family all unharmed offered comfort, but it was no guarantee that they would be successful in any attempt to save her. She hoped they would not put themselves in danger to save her. She also knew she must not give up hope or she would be lost in a quagmire of despair.

Her dreams were both a comfort and a torment. In sleep, there were visions of happiness and love, then a dark cloud would descend, and the joy would be torn away. She would waken panting, then try desperately to remember the pleasurable moments. Forcing herself to hang on to the images of love and family, she determined not to lose courage.

As the weeks passed, Olivia grew more and more impatient with her companions and their constant whining. The food was too spicy, they had to eat with their fingers, the clothes provided were odd and unladylike. Olivia found their behavior exhausting. Luckily, the two slept a great deal and that offered Olivia respite. When the sisters were awake, their grievances were unrelenting.

One day, the annoyance had simmered to boiling and Olivia could no longer contain it.

"Are there no sweetmeats?" Amelia wailed.

"Enough!" Olivia exploded. "We are all suffering the same fate here and your never-ending objections are not helping."

Charlotte wrinkled her nose. "You are not so high and mighty here, *my lady*. We do not have to tolerate your abuse."

Olivia closed her eyes and bit down on her lower lip

to contain her urge to scream. "Have you no idea what really awaits you?"

"You have already attempted to terrify us by insinuating our virtue would be imperiled. But the men have not touched us, and we have food, such as it is, and clean clothes." She looked down her nose in obvious distaste. "Why, they even let us up on the deck from time to time to take the air, as long as we have veils over our faces," she allowed, stating the obvious. "I hate that. The fabric makes it difficult to draw air." She waved her hands in the air to emphasize her point. "I think, although I am very angry at these insults to my person…" Amelia nodded to Charlotte. "…to *our* persons, that it will not be so bad in Morocco as you have described. It might even be an adventure. Why, as I recall, you said those very words when we were first thrust into this horrible room."

Olivia exhaled and pressed her lips together. "Then let me tell you some things I have *not* shared. And the fate of those who make their displeasure obvious."

"Another of your stories. I wonder how much of what you tell us is actually true. I think that when the sultan realizes who we are, we will suffer no indignities of any kind," Charlotte huffed. "I am beginning to believe those women he keeps in his harem are naught more than," she lowered her voice, "whores". She stuck out her tongue as if the very word had an unpleasant taste. "Why, they probably enjoy spending time with the man. Like brood mares."

Olivia took another deep breath and clenched her fists at her sides. Must they be so obstinate? "I suppose I should not bother explaining more, but I could not live with myself if I did not try to educate you in this. Unfortunately, as I have already told you, my family has

23

much experience in these matters, and I am compelled by my conscience to talk some sense into you." Olivia shook her head to focus her thoughts. "As I related to you in the very beginning, your virtue is not in immediate danger. The men on this ship will not touch you under penalty of death. Do you not notice how they do not even look at you when you pass them on the deck? That particular pleasure is reserved for the sultan himself. And he will not hesitate to take whatever he wishes. *Whatever* he wishes," she repeated for emphasis.

"He would force us? Without benefit of clergy?" Charlotte shook her head. "That would be—". She could not bear to even say the word. "Why that does not happen to those of noble birth."

Olivia raised her eyebrows in disbelief. "Who told you that? The sultan is like a god in his country. No one would naysay him. Their lives would immediately be forfeit. And if you become heavy with child, you will no doubt be poisoned by one of his wives. Or, if you fail to conceive, the sultan could decide to give you to one of his soldiers. And that would be a lucky fate."

Amelia looked askance at her. "Even if we believed you, which I am *not* sorry to say, we do not, what is the solution? What do you suggest we do?"

"First, I would offer that you must not be difficult. Cooperate and it might save your life. And when we have gained the trust of our captors enough to relax their vigil, we might just be able to figure out a way to get home."

Both women shrugged simultaneously. "We are all of noble birth. How do you forget that? No ruler would harm us."

"And our father will order our release." Charlotte shook her head as if warding off Olivia's warnings.

"Our families have no power in the world of the sultan. How can I make you understand?" Throwing her hands in the air, Olivia huffed out a breath. In a cooler tone, she continued. "It is doubtful your father will even know your fate, or where you have been taken. Can you not see that?"

Their constant denial of what was happening to them was another source of frustration. Olivia was desperately trying to aid these girls by relating what was to come. And, by attempting to help them, she was strengthening her own resolve to survive and escape. But the more she spoke, the more she seemed to increase their indignation and refusal to accept the reality. Olivia found herself at a loss. How could she help these women when they continued to blindly reject what she offered?

One morning after what had certainly been weeks, a banging on their door roused them early. The ship had slowed and was moving jerkily. A loud clanking confirmed the dropping of an anchor. They were coming into port and the real terror was about to begin. Olivia's veins iced. She knotted her fingers together to cease their quivering. She was quite aware the women had a certain amount of security on the voyage, since she knew the men were sworn to treat them well. Once taken to the harem, however, there was no guarantee of any protection. They were at the whim of Moulay and his wives, especially the first wife. She was known to be very dangerous.

The sisters had, after some time had passed, made a few concessions. They had reluctantly changed into the offered clothing. Obviously, the dirt and smell had finally overcome their reluctance. Their English clothes had been taken from them and they were now all dressed in Moroccan garb. The multi-colored garments were soft and beautiful, but so unlike what they usually wore. No corset bound their ribs and their legs were encased in soft trousers. Embroidered vests added color and delicate brocade slippers covered their feet. And yet, neither would admit the outfits offered more comfort.

Two guards appeared. Neither man seemed pleased by their assigned tasks. One stood guarding the door while the other approached the women. He was attempting to fasten veils across their faces, which Amelia immediately yanked down. "I cannot breathe with that thing on my mouth," she whimpered. "It is enough!"

The man stepped closer to Amelia, his look menacing. Olivia held up her hand to the man and stepped in front of Amelia and replaced the fabric. "Cooperate or it will not go well for you," Olivia hissed.

Amelia made a face at Olivia, but left the piece in place.

The three were led up on deck and lowered into a small boat, which was then ferried to the shore. Then, they were lifted onto the dock and led forward, a soldier ahead and one behind. The two sisters groused constantly, and Olivia prayed they would quieten. She glared at them, but they both lifted their chins and pointedly ignored her.

Each was then directed to a camel with one of their captors already mounted.

Wanting to put on a brave face, Olivia kept her expression neutral. But inside, her limbs had turned to jelly. She was beyond terrified at the possibilities of what lay ahead of them at their final destination. Nausea threatened and she had to swallow hard to keep down the bitter taste.

Charlotte gasped as the man helping her up onto the animal pushed on her bottom. "How dare you?" she shrieked, striking at him. With that, the man withdrew his support and she tumbled to the ground. All those surrounding the women laughed and Charlotte's cheeks turned so red, Olivia thought they may burst. Charlotte stood and raised her chin haughtily in the air, but this time she allowed the guard to assist her without complaint.

A wave of pity washed over Olivia, but she had to admit she was grateful for the distraction. She was trembling so violently, she thought she, too, might fall to the ground.

She had spent much of her time on the voyage counseling herself to remain calm and keep a clear head. One small consolation was John had taught her much of the language used in this exotic land. Perhaps it could be used as her secret weapon. If the others did not know she understood them, she might have a useful advantage. Now, though, when faced with the reality of her new life, she was bereft, the desolation sinking into her bones. Gritting her teeth, she determined to not only survive, but to free herself and find her way out of this hell. Stories from her family had given her knowledge and she must guard it and use it whenever it served.

# Chapter Two

It took the better part of a week for John to hire the ship and the necessary crew. A week of intense study of the language and culture and Tristan felt ready. He burned with impatience to be aboard the ship and on his way.

"You do not need to be fluent. Only enough to let the Sultan know of your *honorable* intentions," Tazim counseled, reassuringly. "But the more you understand, the better prepared you will be for any eventuality. And, the more the foreign tongue is spoken in your presence, the more you will learn."

John frowned, his worry evident. "What if Moulay decides he wants revenge more than he desires the treasure?"

Tazim smiled without mirth. "You spent enough time in Morocco to know Moulay desires wealth more than anything except power. And, he is wise enough to know that wealth is power. And Tristan...I mean the ambassador, here...will not release the treasure until Olivia is safely aboard the ship headed home. Will you? And we have the added benefit of the *treaty*."

"What if you were dead?" Tristan asked flatly, looking directly at Tazim.

Both John and Tazim turned on him, shocked. "What?" they said in unison.

Tristan shook his head. "Not truly. But what if I told the sultan I had witnessed your demise. That you had been boastful that you had outsmarted the sultan and our king was offended that a commoner had stolen from a ruler. He had also viewed this as an opportunity to cement relations with Morocco. He had you executed and confiscated the treasure. And I was tasked with returning it as an offering of peace." Tristan thought about the feasibility of this and was pleased with the logic. "That might have him look upon me with more favor."

"That is not a bad idea," John stated, quirking an eyebrow.

"Thank you for that," Tazim growled, feigning anger.

"If Moulay thinks you have been killed, he will be more likely to leave you alone. And he might just value the returned cache all the more." John nodded, pleased with this conclusion.

"And the proof would be that I have the treasure," Tristan concurred.

"As for the question of his need for revenge against the rest of us? The sultan is an old man now, his glory days long past. I am counting on the fact he has mellowed with age." John sounded hopeful.

"It has only been three years." Tazim's frown communicated his doubt.

"Three years is a very long time when you are in your seventieth decade of life. And he must wish for more alliances to secure his country before he dies, so I am confident that we can buy Olivia's freedom." John's gaze dropped to the ground and Tristan wondered how sure he was of that statement. But they had to have faith their plans would succeed.

"The ship is ready. The new crewmen are loyal to our

family and will defend you. You will have Leo and Felix Roberts, with you as escort, which would only make sense. No ambassador would travel without some men to guard him. And you have assured us more loyal men have not been born, since their family has served yours for so many years. All will help find Olivia and aid in getting you both back home as quickly as possible. Worry not about revenge no matter what has occurred and take no unnecessary chances," John warned.

*No unnecessary chances?* Tristan was not so inexperienced or naïve to believe this was an easy mission. They would probably all die. But taking action was preferred to sitting by and imagining Olivia alone in that terrible place at the mercy of the merciless.

***

It was difficult to focus. Olivia's head was spinning, and her heartbeat was pounding so loud, she feared it could be heard by anyone standing nearby. She dared not even entertain all the possibilities of what was to come next. She tried to swallow, but her throat refused to cooperate. Inhaling deeply, Olivia closed her eyes and prayed. It calmed her and she was able to sit up straighter, even though the swaying of the animal beneath her threatened to unseat her.

The heat was like nothing Olivia had ever experienced. It bore down on her like a heavy blanket, oppressive and alarming in its intensity. The sun pounded, burning her skin, and she had to squint to keep the brightness from hurting her eyes. If she stayed out here too long, would she wither and blow away? Or merely burn up like so much kindling?

The air was so dry, her throat was parched and she desperately wanted some cool water. But she knew there would be no respite, at least until they reached their destination. She was glad the clothing she wore was loose. A corset and a weighty English gown would have been more punishment in this relentless heat.

They traveled through a bustling marketplace, rugs, jewelry and fabrics being bought and sold. The men and woman were all shouting as they made their best bargains. Olivia marveled at the colors and varieties of the offerings and a bit of the excitement around her leeched into her bones and eased some of her tension. That is, until she turned her gaze forward. Ahead of them loomed a palace of mythical proportions. In other circumstances, it would be magnificent. Reminiscent of Versailles, it dominated the landscape, announcing its superiority to all. They slowly climbed the road for a while and more than once Olivia had to adjust her seat to keep from falling. Riding a camel was nothing like riding her beloved horse. They climbed a sloping path of sand that stretched out around them and then the path leveled. Soon, they were entering a courtyard which was like walking into a dream. Gardens filled with lush flowers in vibrant yellow, reds, oranges and purples surrounded them, the fragrances heady and cloying. Olivia kept reminding herself to keep breathing. There were several separate buildings, each with a strangely shaped curved roof. The late afternoon sun painted everything pink and gold and gave Olivia the feeling she was entering a fairytale kingdom. Unfortunately, she knew it was all too real. And, although it was incredibly lovely, she knew the devil himself resided there.

Once the camels stopped, the three of them were

pulled from their perches. Olivia's feet struck the stones with a jolt that rattled her teeth. So much time at sea made it difficult to keep her balance. A tall, dark man stepped forward and looked the three up and down as if they were prize horses ready for auction. She was grateful he didn't open her mouth to check her teeth. He sniffed, then nodded, and another man stepped forward and led the women into a building that Olivia guessed was where the sultan's women lived. The man accompanying them indicated a bench along the corridor wall and the three sat meekly, hands folded demurely in their laps. Even the sisters had the good sense to remain quiet now. The man left them, his disinterest obvious in his blank expression.

"What now?" Charlotte hissed under her breath. "Who is in charge? We must speak to him at once."

Olivia bit her lip. "I know not."

"I thought you knew everything," Amelia sneered.

Olivia turned to face the woman. "It will not help you to take your frustrations out on me. Right now, all we have is each other. As I have told you repeatedly, I am as much a captive as you are. Try to remember that." Her voice was firm, but her tone not unkind.

"She's right," Charlotte said, sitting back. "We must help each other."

Before Amelia could respond, another guard appeared and tilted his head to let them know they were to follow him. The three did as he bade and Charlotte stepped up so she was next to him.

"We must speak to the sultan immediately," Charlotte demanded of the man. He ignored her.

"Excuse me, my sister was addressing you," Amelia spat. She grabbed onto his vest and he stopped. The man glared at her with a look that should have set her hair on fire. She immediately loosened her grasp, dropped her chin and took a step back. She spoke no more.

They were taken along a dark corridor. But although they were out of the punishing rays of the sun, it was still nearly unbearably hot. Did one ever get used to this? Olivia marveled at their surroundings. Even in the dim light, she could discern the floor was inlaid with tiny tiles in a myriad of colors of green and blue. Larger tiles in similar colors lined the walls in intricate patterns. Soft, silky fabric hung from the ceiling, waving in the occasional breeze. In the distance, Olivia could hear women giggling. She supposed some were actually happy to be here. She wondered how that was possible.

The women were each taken to a separate small area curtained off with a silk hanging. Olivia expected some protest, but apparently the sisters had decided to take her advice and not argue. She hoped they would continue to behave appropriately for their own sakes.

Olivia's space looked comfortable, with a bed, table and chair. The covering on the cot was a rich tapestry fabric and the furniture was carved with intricate designs. Under other circumstances, it might have been a lovely apartment. She was wise enough not to be taken in by what appeared before her. She was a prisoner and subject to the will of others and those who might do her much harm. No matter the gilt on the cage, it was still a cage and she would not be deceived.

\*\*\*

Tristan spent his weeks aboard the ship going over the copious notes he had been given by John and Tazim. Although he was not truly fluent in Arabic, he now knew much of the language. The two men had also taught him customs and manners so he would not offend the sultan. And he had been given all the information they had on Moulay Ismail, which Tristan hoped would prove valuable.

Tazim and John had shared with him as much as they knew about the sultan and none of it was encouraging. Sultan Moulay Ismail was not a man to be trifled with. He was known as "The Bloodthirsty" and his cruelties were known far and wide. Some said he had been responsible for the deaths of thirty-six thousand. Including some of his own offspring. Exaggeration or not, he was clearly a man who had no value for life. Tristan could not let down his guard for even an instant.

Moulay was also known to have fathered hundreds of children. His sexual appetites were legendary, and Tristan forced himself not to think about what that might mean for a young woman as lovely and innocent as Olivia. It was no easy feat. Especially when Olivia occupied his thoughts, morning and night. He pictured them together, talking, laughing, stealing kisses. Every memory was bittersweet, since he feared they would be the only ones left to him. If he could not release her and bring her back, there would be no more remembrances. He steeled his thoughts. Defeating ideas led to failure. He needed to concentrate on all they would do when they were reunited. He would marry her; they would have healthy, happy children and grow old together.

He loved her. It wasn't just her exotic beauty that made his blood quicken in his veins and his heart pound. She was kind and sweet and unspoiled, unlike so many of the noble women he had encountered. And he knew she loved him in return. She had chanced the wrath of her family more than once to be with him. She had set aside any doubts he was like his lazy, greedy brother who had died in an attempt to extort money from Moulay's men. Olivia was without judgment, pure of heart, and Tristan would risk anything to see her safely back in his arms and those of her family.

The journey was nearing its end and Tristan gathered the two Roberts brothers with him for a final meeting. Only these two loyal men would accompany him to the palace, while the remaining crewmen would wait onshore at the landing. The sailors would guard the ship until Tristan and the men returned. The crew they had brought aboard were loyal to the Kincaids, Tristan had no doubt they would all give their lives, if not for him, then certainly to save Olivia. As would he. In this he had confidence.

The ship dropped anchor and a small boat was dispatched from the shore carrying two armed men. Tristan handed down a missive to the guards and explained they were to take it to Moulay, as it announced the arrival of the British ambassador. He cloaked his nervousness with an air of authority. Now, he must be patient.

While they waited for the sultan's response, Tristan took the time to check the treasure was secure. The captain, who was to be trusted, had told him of the secret compartment. He lifted out a bracelet of emeralds and diamonds and tucked it into his shirt, then replaced the panel secreted in the floor of his cabin. It was so completely hidden, no one would discover its location unless they knew precisely where to look. He then adjusted his white wig and walked onto the deck, flanked by his two loyal bodyguards.

After a short time, a group of soldiers marched onto the dock, and a small vessel was dispatched and rowed out to Tristan's ship. The first step was a success. The sultan had agreed to allow them to come ashore.

As soon as his feet touched the earth, Tristan knew this was the beginning of a journey that would change his life forever. Hopefully, for the good. He straightened his spine.

Without speaking, one of the soldiers stepped forward, nodded his head and then angled it to indicate Tristan and his two men were to follow. The guard viewed him with his eyes narrowed, his suspicion obvious. They needed to be very careful lest they betray themselves in some way.

Camels were lined up for Tristan and the brothers and they awkwardly mounted.

"It doesn't look like a horse," Leo whispered.

"Let's just hope we don't look like asses," Felix whispered in return.

The attempt at humor did little to ease Tristan's trepidations, but he appreciated the effort.

Precariously perched, trying not to fall and make fools of themselves, they held on for dear life as they were led through the streets to the palace. This must have been the way Olivia was taken. The very thought of her on this journey alone made him sick at heart. He believed her to be strong, but he worried. She, like anyone in her place, could only take so much before succumbing to fear and putting herself in an even more precarious position. *Please, let me be in time to save her.*

They passed through the marketplace and ahead, the palace squatted like a demon daring them to challenge it. And so it began.

\*\*\*

Rousing from a fitful sleep, Olivia heard laughing and water splashing. Memory of where she was came flooding back and she had to make herself not give in to total despair. Her family would not allow her to languish here. They would devise a way to help her. She had to hold onto that with all her heart. But then reality intruded. None of them could come here. They would all be recognized and imprisoned or killed. She immediately tamped down the worry. Her family would come up with something, some plan. She mustn't give up hope. It was all she had now.

Getting up from her cot, she quickly dressed. After so many weeks, the soft blouse and pants no longer felt foreign, and she had begun to truly appreciate their comfort and ease of wear. She ventured out into the corridor to explore. Following the sounds, she found herself in a huge open area. The floor and walls were covered with more of the beautiful tiles. Three fountains were scattered evenly about, each large enough to accommodate ten or twelve. Water sang into the pools from pots held in the arms of naked women carved from stone. Olivia wondered how the sculptors accomplished that feat. Things were indeed new and different in this land. And it could have been appreciated had she not been concerned for her very life. That thought struck trembling into her bones, but she quelled the thought.

Trays groaning with all sorts of fruits and sweetmeats lay on tables along one of the back walls. And everywhere were women. They sat or moved about or danced. Some lay across benches or reclined on chairs. All shapes, all sizes, all different complexions—and most were either naked or in various stages of undress. Olivia was aghast at the display. Shera and Catherine's descriptions of the harem had not included this fact, but Olivia assumed this was to be expected. She also knew the older women and those no longer desirable to the sultan were sequestered in another part of the harem. Were the people here afraid old age was contagious?

The gurgling of the water and the thought of a bath was a siren song Olivia found difficult to resist. But if she were to take off her garments and get into a pool without securing permission, the others would not be pleased. This was a society unto itself and there were rules to follow. She needed to gain acceptance to join in. The key was finding out who was in charge. A few had looked at her with disinterest and went back to whatever amusement was before them. Some glanced with disdain and then turned away. Several glared with open hostility. Nary a smile nor a welcome from the group and nothing to indicate the hierarchy here.

Perching on a bench along the wall, she watched the women before her. They were all beautiful. Some played games, while others plucked at odd-looking musical instruments. Some seemed totally engaged, while others napped or rested on couches, nibbling bits of food. Around the walls, a few men stood at attention, watching the activities. They seemed disinterested in the state of undress and merely kept their eyes straight ahead. These must be the eunuchs, who served as both wardens and protectors of the harem.

After a time, the social structure came to make sense. In addition, Olivia remembered all she had been told by her sister and sister-in-law.

In the largest of the fountains, two women were

being bathed and tended by a flurry of servants who washed them and combed their hair. These must be two of the Kadins. Olivia remembered there were only four in the harem and they were the sultan's favorites. They were massaged and oiled and food was brought to them. To wrong one of the Kadins was to offend the sultan himself and the offender would pay with his or her life.

A few women were being washed in the other two fountains as Odalisques tended to them as well. The Odalisques were divided into two categories. They were either general servants, or they were the most beautiful who were trained as would-be concubines and personal servants for the sultan. The general servants were on the bottom of the pecking order and served any and all the other women in the harem. They could be given to a visitor or one of the favored soldiers or spend one night with the sultan if he so wished, provided they had not been with another man first. Then, they would go back into service to the other women unless, after sleeping with the sultan, they became pregnant and gave birth to a male child. Then they would rise in the ranks.

While Olivia was debating with herself as to her next move, the Caswell sisters appeared at an entrance across the room. Their hands were locked together, and their mouths dropped open as they took in the scene. They immediately tried to retreat. But a guard behind them pushed them deeper into the room. Both were bent over, as if in pain, their eyes red-rimmed and puffy.

Another guard stepped up and took hold of Charlotte's arm and directed her to move forward. She cried out. Amelia didn't wish to release her hold on her sister, but the man wrenched her hand free. Tears streamed down both their faces as Charlotte was led away to one of the fountains. But Charlotte's tears turned to surprise and then consternation followed by pleasure as she was surrounded by several of the servants. It became clear the servants were going to pamper her and she relaxed as they led her about, fussing over her. Ignored, and obviously annoyed, Amelia found her way over to Olivia and plopped down beside her.

They sat unspeaking as Charlotte's clothes were removed and she was bathed, and her hair was washed. Sweet oil was rubbed gently into her skin and her tresses were braided and swept up beneath a silken cloth. She laid down on a table and was massaged, her expression one of delight.

Olivia glanced over at Amelia, who by now was seething with jealousy. *If she only knew they were preparing her sister to meet the sultan, she would not be so envious.*

Charlotte was clearly enjoying the attention. She was actually preening and glanced over at her sister. She was finally being treated as she believed she deserved, and she was pleased.

Amelia, on the other hand, stood up, but before she could move forward and, no doubt, demand equal measure, Olivia grabbed her hand and pulled her back onto the bench.

Amelia snapped her head around and glared at Olivia with such fury, Olivia felt it like a physical blow. How was the woman able to summon such wrath with virtually no provocation? For a moment, Olivia was taken aback, then tightened her grip.

"Sit down," Olivia said through gritted teeth. "Your time will come. There are rules here."

"But I am equal to my sister," she whined. "Am I not

as beautiful? Perhaps even more so?" She narrowed her eyes at Charlotte, then turned back to Olivia. "Why is she favored over me?" She was scowling now.

Olivia released her hold and patted Amelia's hand. What could she say? "Yes, you are even more beautiful. That is why they chose Charlotte first. They save the best for last." It was a simple lie, but it worked to placate Amelia, who reacted with a wan smile. Olivia dared not tell her the truth of what was happening. Besides, what good would it do? They no longer had any say in their fates.

The two sat together quietly for a time and then Amelia, her lower lip now stuck out in a pout, announced she was going back to her room. Still glaring at her sister, Amelia shuffled out of the hall. Olivia was washed in sympathy for Charlotte, but there was naught she could do to protect her.

Charlotte sat up and kohl was applied to her eyes. The dark color was stark in contrast to her pale skin and seemed almost like a death mask. Olivia shivered as Charlotte stood and she was helped into her clothing. No pants today. This was a sheer silky dress that appeared woven from butterfly wings. It concealed nothing and clung to every part of Charlotte's body. Bracelets were slid onto her arms and a soft cap attached to her hair. A veil was attached and placed over the bottom half of her face. Then, a heavy embroidered vest was donned over the dress. Obviously, she could not have her body visible as she traveled from the harem to meet Moulay. Charlotte did not protest any of this initially, but lifted her head, clearly proud of her appearance.

One of the servant girls nodded and two men appeared and flanked Charlotte. It suddenly seemed to occur to the girl what was happening. Had she truly believed the pampering was simply for her enjoyment? Her expression betrayed her utter terror. Charlotte's gaze locked with Olivia for a moment as she passed and Olivia wanted to offer some sort of reassurance, but she knew naught would help. She was as frightened as Charlotte.

Amelia appeared at the entrance at that moment. She was momentarily stunned as she watched Charlotte being led away. After a brief hesitation, Amelia ran headlong toward her sister, but another man grabbed her and held her back. Tears streamed down her face as she watched Charlotte disappear into the corridor, all the while screaming her name. A few of the others watched Charlotte's departure with narrowed eyes. There was no doubt they all competed for the favor of the sultan and Charlotte was nothing more to them than more competition. Olivia guessed this must be a common occurrence. Nausea twisted in her stomach. To be so powerless was beyond horrible.

Olivia stood and held out her arms and the other girl fell against her, her sobs echoing. Olivia patted her back until Amelia was slightly pacified, then led her over to a bench.

A lovely young woman approached them. She wore nothing but a scarf about her waist. Her modesty was protected by her long dark hair, which flowed down in front and covered her breasts. Her eyes were almond-shaped and a deep chocolate brown. She was beautiful, with high cheekbones and full rosy lips. She moved with sensual grace, confident in her loveliness. A slow smile lit her expression, but there was something artificial about it. The smile didn't seem to reach her eyes. No matter. Olivia was grateful for any recognition and kindness.

"Hello and welcome," she said in Arabic.

"Thank you," Olivia responded in English.

Amelia looked to her as if Olivia was suddenly a stranger to her. "You understood her words?" Amelia's eyes widened with astonishment. "You speak this barbaric tongue?"

"My family taught me some of the language they speak here." Olivia turned back to the other woman. "I am Olivia, and this is Amelia." Olivia had thought to keep her knowledge of the language secret, but she might do better if she could converse with the others here.

"I am Sabra. I am allowed to keep this name. But you? You will have to be given a new one."

"I thought as much." Catherine, her sister, had been called Nouria, while her brother John was known here as Kemal.

"You speak Arabic? I am impressed. She," she pointed to Amelia, "definitely has the look of the English. But you could be from anywhere with your dark eyes and hair."

"My knowledge of your words is just enough to get by. I, too, am English. I take after my mother who descended from the Egyptians."

"What are you saying?" Amelia interrupted. "And where are they taking Charlotte?" Her whine was piercing.

Olivia patted Amelia's hand. "I think she may not know, but I will ask when the time is right." Olivia heaved a sigh, certain she need not ask. All but Amelia seemed to know Charlotte's immediate destiny. "Perhaps she was taken to be introduced to the sultan." Understated, of course, but perhaps comforting to the other girl.

"But I want to know for certain. She is my sister and I have a right to be informed where she is going." She

43

thrust her shoulders down to emphasize her words. "Perhaps I should join her. If she is meeting the sultan, then I should be there, as well."

"Amelia, it is not your choice. Please understand that." She tried to be soothing.

"And who are you to determine that?" Her irritation was obvious. Olivia thought it best to say no more.

Although Sabra did not speak English, she was clearly aware of Amelia's impatience. She shook her head. "You seem to understand the customs here. Your companion is not so accepting. It will not go well for her." Sabra put her hand to her chest in sympathy.

"She will learn." Olivia nodded in agreement, praying her words were true.

"She will have to. In the meantime, you must eat." Sabra indicated the tables laden with food along the far wall. "And I imagine you would like a bath. There is not that opportunity aboard a ship."

A bath! Olivia was thrilled. Sabra angled her head and Olivia rose immediately to follow. When Amelia did not move, Olivia reached for her. "You must cooperate. Like it or not. Your very life depends on it."

Amelia just lowered her gaze.

"We are being offered a bath and food. Does that not appeal to you?" Olivia reached out to touch the other's shoulder, but Amelia pulled away.

"You are one of them," Amelia hissed. "I do not trust you." And she slumped further down on the bench.

Olivia decided forcing her would only create an unnecessary commotion, and so she gave up and followed Sabra to one of the tables, leaving Amelia to think about her options here. She thought to lead by example. Amelia and Charlotte had still not understood the possible consequences for their rebellious actions. She hoped Charlotte would try to be obedient now. She hated to think of the possible consequences if the girl continued her resistance.

Olivia's stomach growled and she realized she was starving, and the food looked delicious. Exotic fruits, cakes, nuts and some other things that were totally unfamiliar, Olivia tried a bite of everything. Sabra stood by her side and smiled, clearly pleased that Olivia was partaking of the food. Finally, her hunger sated, Olivia looked to her new friend for direction.

Sabra pointed to one of the pools and, with a gesture down her body, indicated that Olivia was to take off her clothes. Glancing over her shoulder, Amelia was glaring at her in disapproval. Olivia shrugged. She was modest by nature, so she turned her back to the room and, dropping her garments, stepped into the warm scented water. It was heaven. She sank up to her neck and luxuriated. Sabra handed her a bar of sweet-smelling soap and Olivia dipped her head under the water and lathered her hair, as well as the rest of her body. She took her time, then reluctantly rose from the water and wrapped herself into a proffered towel. Only it wasn't Sabra who held the cloth. It was another woman with dark red hair and green eyes.

"Thank you," Olivia instinctively said in English.

"I would say welcome, but this is not a place that is desirable." The woman's soft Scottish burr declared her origins. The woman closed her eyes, then looked heavenward, and Olivia related to her misery. She wondered how many of the women here were abducted from their homes in other countries.

"My name is Maggie." The woman's eyes widened, and she quickly put her hand to her lips. "I mean, my name is Maha."

Olivia smiled. "Both are lovely names." She grabbed her garments and dressed quickly, uncomfortable in her unclothed state.

"I was told Maha means beautiful eyes, since mine are strange here, but it also means wild cow." The woman grinned.

Olivia laughed at this and several of the women turned to look at her as if she had annoyed them.

Maha shrugged. "It will take some time, but you will be accepted here. All the women wish to be favored by the sultan and consider newcomers unwelcome competition." Was there a warning in her tone?

Olivia nodded. "I am Olivia and the woman on the bench there is Amelia." Maha stood with her and helped her dress. It seemed strange to Olivia, but then she was unused to customs here. Once clothed, she plucked up her courage to ask about Charlotte. "Her sister was taken away earlier. Do you have any idea where?"

"Probably for inspection by the sultan. He is old, but still interested in having more children. Word is he has already fathered hundreds."

"I have heard that his first wife does not wish him to have more sons." Olivia inhaled through her nose, fearing she had said something that might be construed as offensive.

Maha leaned in conspiratorially. "It is said the Lala used to poison women when they were with child because she wished her son to inherit the throne. But the sultan killed him years ago. Now, I think she and her minions poison just because they enjoy it."

Olivia gasped and the full weight of her situation landed on her like a stone wall. Danger lurked everywhere here and there was no refuge. Her limbs trembled and tears welled behind her eyes.

Sabra joined them and she could now converse with Maha, since Olivia could interpret. There was something about Sabra that made Olivia uncomfortable, but she set her trepidations aside. She needed to befriend the women in order to not just survive, but also ferret out some weakness that would allow her to escape. Soon, however, Sabra appeared bored and went off in search of some other form of entertainment.

Olivia and Maha spent the remainder of the day together, speaking of inconsequential things, like food and the color of their garments. Maha was occasionally called away to perform tasks for the other women, but she would return to Olivia.

Maha imparted knowledge of their surroundings and its workings, with Olivia learning more about the harem and its rules. Maha was halayik, lowest in rank of the women, since her red hair made her less than attractive in the eyes of the Moroccans. She explained that Sabra was hoping to be a gedikli who were trained in dance, recitation of poetry, the playing of instruments and the erotic arts. Those chosen became personal servants to the sultan, dressing and bathing him, serving his food and providing any other services he required. It was not the same as being a Kadin, but it was well above the station of the halayiks.

Occasionally, Olivia would glance over at Amelia, who looked miserable but still unwilling to participate. After a time, Amelia got up and slouched from the space, presumably to return to her own room. Olivia prayed she would see reason and try to get along here. At least until they could find a way out. The only possibility for escape would be by obtaining information from the other women and that could not be accomplished by rejecting them.

# Chapter Three

Tristan could not help but marvel at the unabashed luxury. The sultan certainly spared no expense in furnishing his palace. Every surface glittered with gold or silver or sparkling gems. Magnificent designs in colorful tile adorned the floors and the walls and the spaces were separated with flowing drapes of silk suspended from the ceiling. Arches graced entryways and gurgling fountains were everywhere. The inner courtyard was covered, like an atrium. The shade made it so much cooler, a welcome relief from the pounding sun outside.

The bed in his apartment was huge and covered in a rich tapestry and decorated with pillows. In fact, cushions were everywhere—in the corners, against the walls, on the chairs and chaises. The rooms were a mass of vibrant hues and light.

Tristan took comfort that the two men he had brought with him from the ship, Felix and Leo Roberts, were trusted completely. Their father had been falsely imprisoned and was sentenced to die. Tristan's father went to the king with proof of his innocence and secured his release. The Roberts' loyalty was assured that day.

Both men were strong, with legs like tree trunks and arms thickened with practice on the field. Tristan, himself, had spent many hours on the training field and was strong and well-muscled, and the three together looked as if they could withstand an army.

The brothers were taken to an adjoining space, but quickly returned to Tristan's side, unwilling to leave him alone.

"The riches here…" Leo began.

"…are unimaginable." Felix finished for him. "I just hope Lady Olivia has found herself in similar circumstances."

"I think there would be no circumstances that would be comfortable if I were a prisoner. What think you?" Tristan fisted his hands, resisting the urge to tear through the palace and find Olivia, even though he knew the harem was in a separate part of the compound.

Both Felix and Leo dropped their heads, their shame apparent. "You are right, my lord," Leo whispered.

"Do not forget the sultan is a monster who kills for the pleasure of it. Blinding us with lavish accommodations may just be his way of getting us to let down our guard." Tristan slammed his fist into his other palm.

"I agree," echoed Felix. "So, what is our next move?"

"Unfortunately, I am certain we must wait until we are summoned. I have no doubt that is the way of things here." Tristan wanted to shout down the walls in his impatience. The sultan would make him wait just to lord his authority. He was at the mercy of Moulay Ismail, just as Olivia was and the thought made him furious.

***

Guards were everywhere and Olivia knew every movement was scrutinized. The women who were here seemed not to notice, but Olivia was acutely aware of the presence of the men. She also knew they had no manly parts, which made Olivia very sad for them. But, otherwise they would not be permitted within the walls of the harem, because there was no worry of molestation. Still, it was unnerving. The women walked about unclothed and the eunuchs took no notice. It was an odd situation and Olivia knew she would probably never become accustomed to it.

Early the next morning, Olivia was sitting on her bed when one of the guards passed by her room. Shock widened her eyes. He was so familiar, she nearly cried out. She jumped toward the entrance, but the man was gone before she could summon him. Had she imagined the familiarity? He so resembled Bekir. Could it be? Bekir had been her brother John's loyal friend and companion when John was in Morocco. It had been Bekir who had seen to her sister Catherine's safe delivery home and the man was now married to Shera's maid, Poppy. So how was it he was here now?

Olivia hoped the man would return so she could know for certain. Bekir had aided her sister. Could he be here to save her, as well?

A few moments later, as if in answer to her wish, the man came back by her doorway. This time she was faster. She jumped out into the corridor just behind him.

"Bekir?" she hissed under her breath. She did not wish to be overheard, for he would certainly be taking a terrible risk if he had returned to this country. He would certainly be thought of as a traitor as it was suspected he had helped Catherine escape. And, how did he manage to get to Morocco ahead of her? How was this possible? It made no sense for him to be here. Had her family sent him? But again, how could he so easily get into the harem? Had no one noticed his absence when he left with Olivia's sister years ago?

The man stopped in his tracks, spun around and his jaw dropped. His dark skin paled.

"What did you say?" he asked in Arabic. His eyes were wide with surprise.

"Bekir? I do not understand. How could you know I would be taken?" Olivia did not doubt Bekir's loyalty, so she was completely confused as to how he would have acquired prior knowledge. Unless…was she wrong? Was he part of this scheme? No, that made no sense. He was happy in his new life and had made it clear on many occasions that he had no love for his past existence in Morocco.

Before Olivia could wonder more, the man moved forward and gently pushed her back into her room, his hand covering her mouth. The action surprised more than frightened her and she took a step back. "How do you know that name?" he whispered in Arabic, then immediately dropped his hand and looked embarrassed that he had touched her. "Please forgive me. But I must know. Why do you address me thusly?"

"Bekir? Of course I recognize you. What is amiss?" She squinted at him. Oh, there was no doubt in her mind she faced Bekir. But something must have transpired to confuse him. Had something happened to his mind? Perhaps if she reminded him of the past?

"You saved my sister by taking her from here and bringing her home. You now live in England at Shera's estate. You are married to my sister-in-law's maid, Poppy." By his puzzled expression, she was certain he had lost his memory or his sanity or both. How did he not know who he was? "What has happened to you?" she asked. Her tone was gentle, since she had no wish to upset the man.

"Who are you?" His face had grown paler.

"Olivia Kincaid." Now she was completely confused. "Do you not know me?"

"Are you related to Kemal?" he asked.

"Of course I am. I am John's sister. We have met many times." She frowned in bewilderment. "What is wrong with you?" Concern quickened her heartbeat.

"How did you get here?" he persisted.

She was trying desperately not to let her exasperation show. She inhaled, praying for patience. "I was taken from my home and brought here. I can only guess it was Nabil's men and they must have attacked my family. How else could they have stolen me away without anyone noticing?" She coughed back a sob. "I pray the evil men did no harm to them." Tears filled her eyes at the thought of what may have happened to those she loved.

"Nabil is a terrible man. There is no limit to what he would attempt to further himself with the sultan." Enmity sparked from his eyes.

So, he could recall Nabil. "There is so much he has done to hurt my family. Including arranging my kidnapping, for I have no doubt he is the one responsible."

The man nodded in sympathy, then crossed his arms over his chest. "Do not worry. I will protect you." His stern countenance reinforced his commitment. Olivia did not know what to think. Bekir had just vowed to protect her, but he seemed not to know her identity. Or even his own. Or remember any of the past three years.

But then he tilted his head. A thought seemed to penetrate, and a grin lit his face. "Married? Is he happy?"

Olivia shook her head. "What?" She was totally confused. "Who?"

The man smiled, showing even white teeth. "Bekir is my twin brother."

Shocked, Olivia's eyes widened. "You are not Bekir? He has a twin?"

"Many years ago, I was captured by the sultan's

soldiers to become a eunuch. No one volunteers, you see." His lips curved slightly at the attempt at humor. "My genitals were taken and I was buried in the ground up to my neck. A man is supposed to remain there for three days afterward. That is how it is done here. If you live, you work in the harem. If you die…" He shrugged.

"But who could survive such a travesty?" Her stomach roiled at the images conjured.

"Enough manage to survive. I was near death when my brother found me. He dug me up on the second day and took my place. I was able to escape and heal. I was coming back to free Bekir when one of my friends informed me he had recently disappeared. So, I stepped in before he could be missed by anyone of import. And I did not mind returning for my own reasons." Grim determination set his jaw.

"But he was not…?"

"No. He had to be most careful no one discovered he still had his manhood. But your brother knew the truth."

"Oh." She digested all this for a moment. "Then what is your name?"

"I am Braheem. The name means 'the father of a multitude', which all here find amusing." He shook his head. He did not seem to find the name witty, however.

Relief flooded through her like a cooling breeze. "Thank you."

He stiffened and frowned in consternation, clearly embarrassed by her show of gratitude. She released her hold and he took a step back. "I have done nothing yet."

"You are here, and you are Bekir's brother. I am no longer so alone. That is enough for now. Just to have an ally in this place."

"What of the women that arrived with you? I heard there were three of you. Are they family, too?"

"No. They were taken separately. I tried to explain what it was like here, but they do not trust me. And I fear they do not recognize the seriousness of their situation."

"That is indeed dangerous."

"One of the women, Charlotte, was taken to the sultan yesterday. Do you have any news of her fate?"

"I will see what I can learn. There are no secrets in the harem, so it should not be difficult. But worry not, I shall soon return." And he slipped out.

Her new knowledge filled Olivia with joy. Bekir's brother was here! His twin. Braheem said he would protect her, and Olivia felt so much safer. Her oppressive sense of desolation eased as calm radiated through her veins.

***

Tristan glanced in the mirrored glass as he passed it. He stopped and stared. Who was this odd-looking man? The blue eyes were his and the cut of his jaw, but the terrible white wig perched on his head looked ridiculous, as did the odd mustache. He shook his head. It mattered not, so long as he could find Olivia and rescue her. And so far, no one had sounded an alarm because they recognized him from the attack in the woods.

Two men with bare chests and odd flared white pants held up with embroidered belts waited outside his door to escort him. The costumes in this country were so different and would have looked silly if not for the vicious swords hanging off the men's waists. Felix and Leo flanked him, but one of the sultan's men indicated with a palm up the two were to remain. Both Leo and Felix both took a step forward in protest, but Tristan shook his head. He assumed he was to be taken to Moulay and now was not the time to defy protocol. Tristan believed the sultan's curiosity as to Tristan's mission would keep him and his men safe for now.

Tristan followed the guards down one corridor after another, past many rooms with high ceilings and tiled arches and finally out into a magnificent sunlit courtyard. Flowers bloomed in vibrant bunches that scented the air and fountains sang gentle songs in harmony with the exotic birds. But out in the open the sun was merciless. Looking around, Tristan saw a group of servants awash in sweat and he assumed it was from the harsh rays of the sun. But looking more closely, something else was transpiring. Something sinister. It was then he noticed several guards hanging back behind the men, their hands on their swords.

In contrast to the beautiful, calm surroundings, many men were rigidly lined up in a half-circle along the edges of the paved area where the tiles melted into the sand. By the fear emanating from them, the men, too, wished to dissolve into the landscape. Distress exuded from them like a sour odor. In the center, a tall, slender man dressed in a red robe paced back and forth. Tristan had been warned that when Moulay wore red, someone died. And, clearly this was Moulay Ismail himself. In his hand flashed a deadly scimitar, its wicked edge gleaming the promise of death. Tristan stopped at the entrance to the open space and waited to be recognized, his pulse screaming in his ears. His guards stayed next to him, clearly having no wish to move forward either. Tristan inhaled slowly and blinked away the bright light. The heat shimmered around him and sweat now dampened his clothes. Showing fear was the worst possible emotion, so he wiped away the visible perspiration, straightened his spine and squared his shoulders. He quickly scanned the line of trembling souls looking for any sign of Olivia. But there were no women present.

Moulay ignored Tristan and continued his march up and down the ranks. From the way he carried himself, Tristan could tell he was still a vigorous man, even though he was in his seventieth decade. His skin was dark and his features well-formed. The word that came to Tristan's mind was formidable.

Finally, the sultan stopped his pacing as two servants approached and entered the circle, dragging behind them a woman who appeared more dead than alive. Tristan's heart stopped. He was terrified he had come too late and that the woman was Olivia. Endless seconds passed until the scarf covering her head slipped and he caught sight of her blonde hair. Relief flooded through him.

A closer look at the woman and his respite turned to disgust. Her clothes were stained dark with gore and her head lolled forward. Clearly she had been much abused, her pale skin marked with a myriad of bruises, her breath coming in painful gasps. She would have fallen to the ground had she not been supported by the men.

The sultan latched onto her right arm by the elbow and held it up. It was then Tristan noted with revulsion that her right hand was missing. Fresh blood covered her arm and dripped onto the stones. The sultan announced the woman had attempted to slap him. The men had the good sense to appear horrified, their mouth dropping open. The idea of anyone daring to strike the god that was Moulay Ismail was unthinkable, unspeakable. Moulay turned and screamed into the women's slackened face. He was asking her if she was sorry. Her eyes flickered open and she showed no sign she was aware of anything that was happening. Her lack of remorse infuriated him, his face darkening and his scowl pinching his eyes together. A whish through the air and her head hit the ground and bounced. Red flecks sprayed across the stones and Tristan had to press his hand to his mouth to keep from vomiting. Unfortunately, he raised his gaze and saw the sultan's pleased smirk at his action. Tristan was unnerved to his core.

He had been warned of Moulay's capacity for atrocity, but hearing of it and seeing it were two quite different things. He knew then he had led a sheltered existence until now. Rescuing Olivia was his idea of the fairy tale—the white knight charging in on his stallion and scooping up the fair maiden. But this was not a children's story. Before today, he could not have conceived of so hideously bloodthirsty an act if he had not witnessed it for himself. He was shaken to the marrow of his bones, but he would not be defeated by it. Now, more determined than ever, he had to get Olivia out of this hell.

Servants scrambled to remove the woman's body and her head. Another cloak was brought to the sultan and he slipped off the blood-stained one. Fastening the proffered yellow cloak, he was acting as though he had just come out to take the air, so nonchalant were his actions. Moulay then turned to Tristan and grinned. It was the smile of the devil himself and the air was torn from Tristan's lungs. First, he was frozen in place and then he had to suppress his urge to run. Instead, he tightened his muscles to control the trembling and lifted his head. He would not act the weak-kneed nobleman. It was time to step up. But he must tread carefully, lest his emotions come to the fore and allow him to be outsmarted.

"Oh, Great One. It is an honor to be in your presence." Tristan spoke in Arabic as the sultan lifted an eyebrow at him. He nearly choked on the words, but he had to do whatever it took to gain this man's philanthropy. He bowed his head to show his respect, but he also used it as a moment to compose himself.

Moulay Ismail swung his hand to the side, palm up, to let Tristan know he was to follow. The ranks closed behind them as the sultan strode into the building and down a short hallway which opened into a huge room. Color and rays of light filled the space and glistened on the walls which, like the other rooms and hallways, were decorated with multi-colored tiles in intricate patterns. The ceilings here, too, rose to lofty heights, accented with arches in each corner of the room. A throne covered in gold and cushioned with richly embroidered pillows at the far end squatted atop three steps and dominated the room. The sultan took his place on the elevated seat and pointed to some pads on the floor at his feet. Tristan understood he was to kneel at the foot of the man. There was no mistaking the sultan's need to rise above.

The sultan settled on his cushions as a servant appeared with a tray of fruit and nuts, bowing deeply as he held forth his bounty. Moulay motioned the man away.

Tristan took this opportunity to take measure of the ruler. He did not reflect the years as one might expect. His features were angular and sharp, his lips narrow and his skin smooth with few signs of age. A forked beard and full mustache did not soften the countenance. His eyes were dark and reptilian, with a coldness that drove into Tristan's soul. There would be no mercy from this tyrant. His military successes were noteworthy, and his slaves were very loyal, but no doubt this was due to the man's reign of terror, inspiring fear to gain devotion.

"So, ambassador, you speak our language." The

sultan's face remained impassive. Did this fact please the man?

"Not as well as I should," Tristan replied humbly. "It is indeed a lyrical tongue."

Moulay inhaled through his nose, then blew out the breath. Tristan could not discern if the sultan was annoyed or pleased. "What have you brought us?" Moulay prodded.

Tristan allowed a small smile to raise the corners of his lips. "Riches, Great One. Just as my missive said."

Moulay raised an eyebrow. "Our own property? Your letter stated you had found the treasure the criminals stole from us."

"Such an unforgivable affront, to steal from your majestic self. And yes, I have brought back the property that belongs to you. That and the offer of so much more." Tristan kept his voice calm, his determination to accomplish what he came for overcoming any trepidation.

Moulay raised an eyebrow. "And how do we know you do not deceive us?" Tristan nodded and reached into a pocket. Instantly, he was surrounded by soldiers. He held up his hands, then very slowly extracted the glittering piece he had carried with him. One of the guards grabbed it and presented it to the sultan, who eyed it critically. After a moment that took a lifetime, Moulay waved the guards back and nodded.

"And the man who possessed this before you?"

"Dead, Great One. I have seen to it. Without doubt his continuing to live after betraying you would not be acceptable." The lie slipped out easily. "I supported my king in his decision to end the man's life."

Moulay nodded again and almost smiled. "I only wish it had been by my sword." He shrugged, forgetting for a moment the royal pronoun. "Where is the rest?"

"Safe. And as I am certain you expect, I was hoping we could enter into some negotiation." Tristan tried to keep his tone even. So much was at stake. "I understand you are a master of that art."

Moulay stood up and flung his arms wide. His face darkened with his anger and his gaze shot daggers at Tristan. "You dare bargain with us over our own belongings?" His voice had risen to a scream that seemed to shake the walls. Two guards leapt toward Tristan again, their hands on the swords at their waists, looking to the sultan for direction. Tristan forced himself not to react. "Oh, no, Great One. Of course, your jewels will be returned to you post-haste. It is not my intent to withhold what rightfully is yours and yours alone. But, as for the rest… From my letter you know I have other offerings that are up for discussion."

Moulay calmed and reclaimed his seat. The guards backed off and returned to their places along the walls. "Go on," Moulay encouraged. He was suddenly almost friendly in tone and his mercurial moods were unsettling. "Do tell us more of this treaty you have brought."

"A trade agreement with England. One that will be most profitable for you and your country. And it will gain you more of the recognition you so deserve in my country."

Moulay sat, his expression impassive, but his dark eyes sparkling. "We have such agreements with France." He raised an eyebrow in challenge.

"Yes, but can one ever have too many friends?" The sultan was a man of extraordinary cleverness. But Tristan was also determined not to be outdone by this monster. With such intellect, the sultan also possessed greed and the desire for control and Tristan counted on these flaws to use against the man. "And, my government has much power in her military. So, again, can one ever have too many allies?"

The sultan's forked beard lifted as he sucked in his cheeks. "And we suppose your government would support us out of the goodness of her heart?"

"First, may I say my government has nothing but the greatest respect for you and your country. Seeing it for myself, I can appreciate what a magnificent work you have accomplished just in this palace alone." Tristan waved his arms around to emphasize his words. "But, mine is a great nation, as well. And we would offer you what we expect in return. An exchange of goods and ideas. And, all we require, nay ask, is an act of friendship on your part."

Moulay nodded knowingly. "And this act for our—friendship?" The eyebrow lifted again. "What is it your government desires from us?"

"Release of a certain captive. A female that was taken from England."

"A woman?" Disbelief dripped from Moulay's tone. "Who could so value a woman? You truly expect us to believe you?"

"Oh, the woman herself is of worth only in that she carries a royal heir." He had thought of this on the voyage. There was no doubt Moulay understood the importance of heirs, even if he had ended the lives of many, including his own offspring.

A slow smile lifted Moulay's lips. The pleasure was reflected in his eyes. "And so we have a valuable hostage?"

Tristan's spine straightened. He had not meant to bring the sultan something more to bargain with. He was on thin ice and knew to trod carefully. "You have what amounts to an invasion and an act of war if she is not released."

Moulay stroked his grizzled jaw with his knuckles for

a few moments. Then he shrugged. "And for the release of a woman you will return our treasure and offer us future status as an ally of Britain?" He smiled and a chill traveled up Tristan's spine. "She must be very valuable indeed."

Tristan watched the sultan for anything that might give away his thoughts, but he was disappointed. Moulay's face was without expression. "Releasing her would be deemed a great act of friendship on your part. My king appreciates such actions and is happy to show our country's gratitude. An amicable relationship between Morocco and England will be as good as done when I have boarded my ship with her."

The sultan did not respond, but merely shook his head and Tristan flushed as his panic rose. Again, he could not read what was going on in Moulay's thoughts and he was at a disadvantage.

"Guards!" The sultan's voice echoed as several men grabbed Tristan and pulled him to his feet. Sweat broke out on his forehead and he closed his eyes in defeat. This was a disaster. He had failed miserably and now he and, most likely Olivia, would die for this calamity.

"Take this man to his apartments and see that he and his men have all they require for their comfort."

Tristan almost slumped in relief at the sultan's words. His head still pounded, but his chest allowed him to draw breath again. He had not shown weakness and he was relieved.

"Thank you, Great One. I await your decision and your pleasure." Tristan hoped Moulay did not notice the tremor in his voice.

***

Braheem tapped on the wall of Olivia's room very early the next morning. She blinked awake and jumped from her bed to greet him. His expression told her the news he brought was not good.

"What is it?" she asked without preamble.

Braheem lowered his head. "Your friend is dead," he whispered.

Immediately, she knew he referred to Charlotte. What had she done to offend Moulay? Something terrible enough to lose her life. Although here, something terrible could be the most minor transgression. Bile rose into her throat. "Oh, no. How did it happen?" She pressed her hand to her lips as tears burned her eyes.

"She apparently tried to slap the sultan when he fondled her."

Olivia gasped. She had warned them. Why did Charlotte not heed her words? Olivia shook her head and the sobs constricted her throat. It took her a moment to speak. "I feared her lack of humility would be dangerous." And suddenly the reality of her situation struck her like a blow to the chest. She inhaled and swallowed. "I must inform her sister."

Braheem pressed his hands to his chest. "I am sorry."

"As am I." Olivia had failed, and it pressed on her.

Charlotte was spoiled, but she did not deserve a fate such as this at the hands of that bloodthirsty demon. Olivia wondered if only she had tried more forcefully to warn her, Charlotte might have survived. But Olivia knew in her heart she had done all she could. The other woman would simply not heed her advice.

Olivia could only conjecture how she would react in a similar situation. Her gorge rose at the thought of that terrible old man touching her, but would she value her chastity more than her life? She supposed she would not truly know until faced with the decision, but she prayed it would never come to that.

Braheem stood by quietly as Olivia composed herself and wiped away her tears.

"There is more. Did you know your country has sent an ambassador to obtain your release?"

"An ambassador?" Suspicion mingled with curiosity. "My country sent an ambassador?" But that made no sense. The king would not trouble himself with such matters. Olivia was thoroughly confused.

"The man says your condition," and Braheem's gaze dropped to her stomach, "is due to the attentions of a nobleman. A nobleman who is a friend of your king."

Olivia frowned. "My condition? Oh," she said, as realization struck. Brilliant. If it was thought she carried a noble heir, especially if the sire was a man of high rank, the sultan might believe she had value to her country and release her more easily. She grinned. "The ambassador is an ingenious man."

He narrowed his eyes. "Are you not…?"

Could she trust him? He was Bekir's twin, true, but would he betray her? He was Bekir's brother and he had voiced loyalty to her. She would have to trust someone. "The attentions I have received from *a nobleman* would not produce a child." She grinned. "But who is this ambassador?"

"I know not. But I have no doubt you will find out soon enough. Just remember, I will give my life to protect you."

"But why? Why risk so much for me?"

"You have given me a great gift in the knowledge that my brother is alive, free and happy." And with that, he disappeared down the corridor.

Thrilled at the possibility someone had indeed been sent to take her from this place filled her with joy and optimism. But who was this ambassador? She was sure the king knew naught of this, but it was a very clever ruse. One the sultan could not easily discredit. But did the ambassador have any idea who he was dealing with? She searched her thoughts. Who would risk his life for hers? It could not be John or Tazim. They would both be instantly recognized. And, although she knew how much her father loved her, she doubted her brother would stand by and let him run such a risk. Who then? Tristan was sorely wounded, and wouldn't the men who beat him recognize him once he showed his face here? Who then would be her champion? Her heart fluttered at the idea that someone was indeed here for her. There was hope and she clung to it with every fiber of her being.

Her thoughts returned to Amelia. How was she going to tell the fragile girl her sister was gone, never to return? Olivia decided she needed to go looking for Amelia soon, no matter how unpleasant the task. Olivia was also aware Amelia must be cautioned not to act similarly. But Olivia was in no hurry. The thought of relating such terrible news made her limbs heavy with apprehension and grief. She could only imagine how she would feel if something happened to Catherine or Shera. The thought made her light-headed.

First, she sought out the other girl's room and was surprised to find it empty. She wandered down the corridor to the main area and there was Amelia, sitting on the edge of one of the bathing pools. She was apart from the other women, gazing into the water and trailing her fingers in its depth. Misery covered her like a shroud.

Olivia approached slowly. Amelia would most likely

not be pleased to see her, and when she delivered the news, the girl needed a quiet place to mourn. Olivia thought to take her back to her apartment.

"Amelia?"

The girl looked up, a scornful expression creasing her brow. "What is it?"

"I came bearing news. But I think you and I should retire to my room." Olivia kept her tone gentle. She reached out her hand to Amelia, but the other woman looked at it disdainfully.

"What news? You seem to know so much." Sarcasm dripped from her tone.

"I am not your enemy." She drew in a deep breath. "I fear something has happened to Charlotte." She bit her lower lip.

Amelia jumped up and angled her face close to Olivia's. "Where is my sister? What have you done with her?" Her voice was loud and high-pitched. It was in that moment that Olivia realized she had become the recipient of all of Amelia's anger and fear. This was not simply distrust; it was naked rage. She could not fathom a reason why, except perhaps it was easier to choose a scapegoat.

"I am not your enemy," Olivia repeated, even more gently this time. The women around them had surreptitiously moved closer to watch the drama unfold. Olivia could feel their eyes upon her, and it made the hair on her nape rise.

"Come with me." She did not want to deliver the information so publicly. Amelia was allowed some privacy in this.

"Just tell me," Amelia spat.

Olivia shook her head in defeat and sank down next to her. Amelia remained standing, glaring down at her.

Olivia hesitated, then firmly decided this terrible news would be better coming from a sympathizer. Just because Amelia was angry with her was no reason for her to respond in kind. "Your sister will not be returning here."

Amelia's face paled even more than usual. Her mouth opened and emitted a gurgling sound. Then, she snapped it closed and glared at Olivia, eyes narrowed. "What does that mean? What is truly happening, since I am certain you know?" Poison oozed now. "After all, you understand the primitive language of these people."

Olivia was in it now and needed to do what she intended. "I was told the sultan tried to…touch her…and she raised her hand against him." Olivia closed her eyes at the vision she conjured.

Amelia's eyes widened and she nodded an affirmation. "As she should have done. Unlike you, my sister is a lady who does not tolerate an assault on her person. Good for her." Amelia seemed very proud of Charlotte's actions.

Olivia grabbed Amelia's forearms and gently pulled her down onto the edge of the pool. Amelia scowled at her with defiance.

"Amelia, she has been killed." The words tore from Olivia's chest as she spoke them.

Amelia's reaction caught her totally off guard. She laughed. It began as a giggle, then built to a throwing back of her head until it nearly reached hysteria. Olivia gaped at her. The other women took steps away from the now wild creature before them.

Finally, Amelia calmed and looked Olivia directly in the eye. "Do you truly think I would believe this so-called sultan would have the nerve, the gall, to harm a lady of the realm?" She shook her head in disgust. "Where is Charlotte? When will she be returning? And why would you be so cruel to make such a terrible falsehood. What kind of a person are you?"

Olivia leaned closer to the other woman. Amelia scooted away to put distance between them. "Amelia, this place is not like home. I have tried to tell you. Their rules are not like ours. The sultan is considered a god here. No one would naysay him for any reason. Your sister attempted to strike him. Do you understand? She had to pay with her life."

Olivia watched Amelia's face in horrified fascination as the madness took hold. "I should scratch out your eyes for making up such a hideous lie. Just wait until Charlotte returns and we will see you severely punished," Amelia spat out.

Olivia was unsure how to react, but her body flinched as if she had been physically attacked. She tensed her muscles and sat very still as Amelia rose and straightened her spine. In one swift movement, she thrust her hands at Olivia's chest and Olivia tumbled backward into the water. Choking at the unexpected assault, Olivia scraped her hands along the bottom as they broke her fall. Warm water filled her nose and she coughed. She lifted her head, and still stunned, she managed to sit up in the pool as Amelia stomped from the room. The women around them ducked their heads to unsuccessfully cover their laughter, then turned their backs.

Olivia inhaled deeply and let the pounding of her heart ease. She stood slowly, soaked to the skin. Maha ran up to her and offered a towel.

"I will get you some dry clothing," she said.

Olivia barely heard her. She was still bewildered at

the unwarranted attack. Amelia had completely lost her sanity and Olivia was awash in sympathy for the other woman.

Later, she would try and speak to her again, when the shock had receded. Perhaps Olivia could talk some sense into her. Unless her mind had so closed off that there would be no way to reach her. The thought of that made Olivia ache.

# Chapter Four

Tristan paced the floor, his nerves taut. He had no idea what was to happen next and he was acutely aware he had no control in this country. He and his men could be killed, or tortured, as easily as have their demands met. The sultan could order his ship searched and kill his men. Or he could acquiesce to Tristan's demands and set them free. But he feared that would be too easy.

One thing Tristan knew for certain. He had no intention of standing idly by while the sultan exercised his will. At night and again before dawn broke, he slipped out and explored the corridors. The palace was like a maze and it took intense concentration to map it in his mind. He talked to any of the guards that would speak to him and quickly learned which of the areas were private and which were public. He found the exits, observed the customs, and determined the hierarchy. He payed attention to who came and who went. The sultan's suite occupied the entire north section and he peered around corners to determine who guarded him and how many.

He worried over Olivia and her fate. Had she been abused? Was she at risk now or safe behind the harem walls? Was there such a thing as safety in this place? The thought tormented him. His fists clenched at the idea someone had damaged even the tiniest hair on her head.

And his helplessness was compounded by the waiting. A day passed, then another. Now, it was mid-afternoon of the third day, and they had heard naught from Moulay.

As the time had passed, Tristan and his men had been brought trays of exotic foods he could not taste. Women appeared to escort them to baths, where they immersed in warm water smelling of a tantalizing musk and something called patchouli. And Tristan barely noticed. He and his men were coddled and tended and there was no pleasure in any of it. Tristan only wanted Olivia and then escape for them all. And until he could see her with his own eyes, and confirm she was safe, he would not rest.

They were sitting in Tristan's apartments and it was early morning. Breakfast had just been delivered, but Tristan had no appetite.

"It is most pleasant here," said Felix, popping an apricot into his mouth. "And although the food is delicious and the service amazing, I have no doubt it is like a dangerous web."

"Indeed," Tristan agreed. "Beautiful but a deadly trap."

"I agree. One of the women who bathes us speaks our language and she has peppered me with questions. I have no doubt she reports to the sultan all that she hears." This from Leo, who pushed out breath. He turned to Felix. "I just hope your wife never hears of a naked woman having her hands on you."

"*I* would never tell her." Felix glared at his brother.

"Nor I, brother," Leo affirmed, grinning and pushing a finger into Felix's shoulder.

"What was said between you and the women?" Tristan prodded, ignoring their banter.

71

"Worry not, my lord. We have betrayed nothing." Leo's tone was defensive.

"I did not mean to question your loyalty," Tristan assured him. "I was just curious as to the questions they asked you."

Leo shrugged. "What do we want, why are we really here. I suppose she thinks to seduce the answers from us." He rolled his eyes. "I do have to admit, the women here are truly lovely." It was said as an afterthought. Tristan could not help but agree, although he only had eyes for Olivia. Such as that was love.

"Like spiders that mate and then kill?" Felix suggested, grabbing his throat with both hands.. "I trust them not. In fact, I trust no one here."

"What is taking so long? I do wish they would send for us so I could find Olivia," Tristan huffed. "This waiting is driving me to distraction." But he was certain the sultan was keeping him waiting to gain an advantage. And let them know who was in charge.

As if hearing his words, two soldiers appeared at the entry. They motioned for Tristan and held up their hands to indicate the other men were to remain.

"It is not wise to go unescorted," Leo hissed under his breath.

"What choice have we? It is their way or risk enmity, which we cannot afford. I will be fine." Tristan hoped his words proved true. The three of them were no match for a palace full of soldiers. If the sultan wished them dead, it would come to pass and there would be nothing they could do.

Tristan was led down another series of corridors and finally into a small reception area. One of the guards indicated a bench and Tristan nodded, then sat down, his blood churning and his heart thrumming against his ribs. He tried to quiet his thoughts and remain passive, although his only desire was to jump up and throttle these men within an inch of their lives. They, of course, were only following orders. The last bastion of the cowardly or those who lived in daily fear for their very existence.

Two more guards marched into the space, a veiled woman between them. Tristan immediately stood up and it took him only a moment to realize it was Olivia who stood staring at him over the fabric that covered the lower half of her face. Joy that she was alive and appeared healthy filled him and it was all he could do not to leap over to her and gather her in his arms. Instead, he controlled his desire by fisting his hands and digging his nails into his palms. Somehow, he managed to school his features to suppress his elation.

A thousand emotions flashed in her eyes, but she was canny enough to reveal nothing to her captors. It was clear she recognized Tristan immediately, even with the terrible wig. He could see her pleasure in her gaze at the sight of him, but she stood placidly between the two soldiers, waiting.

"My lady," he said, and swept a bow. "I am hoping you fare well. It cannot be easy in your condition."

A smile lit her eyes.

Now he was confused. Did she know to what he referred? But how was that possible? He had only just thought of it before they landed here. "The child you carry," he stated pointedly.

She blinked rapidly, inhaled and nodded her understanding. He was, as ever, amazed at her cleverness. Or was what he had heard true? Were there no secrets in the palace?

73

"And I assume you are the ambassador sent to retrieve me," she said quietly. She lowered her chin and dropped her gaze. Tristan thought it a wise move, so she didn't betray her emotions.

"Yes, my lady. The Duke is most anxious as to your welfare."

"Is he? And has he paid a ransom?" She shifted from foot to foot and he could tell her anxiety was gnawing at her.

"Let me assure you he has put the necessary elements in place to secure your safe release."

"And he is well?" she asked pointedly.

"Quite well, my lady," Tristan responded, slightly confused.

"And *his family*? They are well?" she asked.

Now he knew she asked after the welfare of her own loved ones. "Again, quite well, my lady."

He saw her sigh with relief. "That is good to know. When do we leave?" He could hear raw hope.

"We are at the pleasure of the sultan, but I cannot imagine it will take too much time to complete our arrangements."

Before she could respond, the soldiers took hold of her arms and guided her from the room. Watching her walk away, Tristan was bereft that she was being taken away. He reminded himself she was undamaged. That alone cheered him. The sight of those soldiers touching her enraged him, but he was grateful she immediately understood his strategy. He had confidence she would return to the harem and go on with the charade that she carried a babe.

***

When the soldiers had first escorted her down the hallway and out of the harem, her heart had lodged into her throat. Was it her turn to be taken to the sultan? What of the ambassador? God only knew what was in store for her. Her limbs had shaken and her head spun. She had been only vaguely aware of the bright sunlight pouring over her as they walked down a stone path. Then, she was directed through a series of doors into the palace and she prayed she would not faint. Her breath came in short gasps now and she bit her lower lip to control her panic. They stepped through a curtain and suddenly she was in a huge room, still flanked by her guards. She lifted her eyes, expecting to see Moulay, and joy had erupted in her chest.

Tristan was here! He had come for her. He was obviously the English ambassador. Olivia's excitement knew no bounds. Her spirit flew wild with hope, even though her body was still held captive. It was all she could do not to run into Tristan's arms when she saw him, but that would have been dangerous. Giving these people any more information than was absolutely necessary could prove dangerous. And she was supposed to be carrying another man's babe.

She listened as Tristan confirmed his strategy in English. How resourceful he was. Carrying a noble's child would assure her better treatment in the harem and hopefully protect her from the advances of the sultan. As she was marched away from Tristan and down the corridors, she forced down a giggle, but it came out as a choking sound and the soldiers regarded her as if she had lost her mind. Now all she had to do was carry on the pretense until he could manage her release, which should take no time at all now. No doubt, the sultan did not wish to inflame an English noble. Moulay Ismail might be a god in his country, but he had to know he was no match for England if it came to a conflict.

Their exchange had been terse and she prayed it betrayed no emotion, although her insides were a maelstrom of happiness and fear for his safety. Too soon, she had been ushered from the room and she had been desperate to turn back, but it would be a mistake. She drew comfort from the words he spoke of the "duke's" family. He must know she meant her own people and he confirmed they were well. Relief was like balm.

Olivia was taken to her room and she sank onto the cot. Breathing easier than she had since she had been taken, Olivia realized she must find a way to convince the other women she was with child.

She busied herself finding a few scarves to tuck into her belt. The loose clothing she wore revealed little, so she would not have to explain why her stomach had appeared flat before. And when she had bathed, her modesty had her turning her back to the room, with her arms covering her, so no one could have observed her stomach. Enhancing her belly now would assure there would be no question as to her 'condition'. She calculated she should be at least four or five months along.

It took three scarves and a shirt, but finally she was satisfied she exhibited the proper amount of curve. She stroked the mound, wondering what it would feel like to actually carry a child. Tristan's child.

Satisfied, she sat back down on her bed and thought about the man she had fallen in love with. The bravest of them all, who had risked everything to come here for her. Her chest filled with butterflies and she hugged herself, imagining it was he who held her. She missed his kiss and his touch. Of course, they had done no more, but his demonstrations of affection in the past convinced her of his devotion. And now, coming here to rescue her had left no doubt of his commitment.

Months ago, while they were both still in England, he had said he intended to marry her, but he was hoping for her family's approval. His half-brother had conspired with the sultan's evil miscreants and paid with his life. But her family did not trust Tristan because of what his brother had done. But, after this, they would not deny him.

She eased back against the pillows and imagined the wedding. She would float down the aisle in a beautiful dress. Blue. It would be a pale blue silk. Her hair would be intertwined with flowers. When she approached, her handsome groom would catch his breath and they would smile at each other with all the love in their hearts. It would be perfect. And then, later, when she truly carried a child, it would be hers and Tristan's, conceived in love and binding them more tightly together.

She drifted off to sleep, thoughts of love and joy filling her heart.

***

Olivia had no sooner been escorted from the space, then Tristan was led into another area with low tables, the floor covered with cushions. Moulay sat ensconced on pillows set up on a dais placing him higher than those he received. A long, low table squatted in front of the man.

Tristan strode over to the ruler, his head held high, but not too high. He did not wish to communicate a lack of respect. Soldiers, their spines rigid, stood around the walls. The sultan was smiling, but it did not reassure Tristan of the other man's good intent. His cold, black eyes reminded Tristan of a snake. A very ruthless, calculating snake. Also, Moulay wore yellow and the color set Tristan's teeth on edge. Any color but green warned of a risk. Tristan had witnessed for himself this was a man who took pleasure from the pain of others. And then was immediately able to forget about it. Human life meant nothing to him. Tristan must tread very carefully.

A gesture with Moulay's hand indicated Tristan was to sit on the other side of the table, which would put him again below the sultan's feet. The nobleman in him rebelled, but this was not a time for false pride. He sat on a cushion and leaned back, his weight on his forearms, and crossed his legs. He hoped he appeared relaxed.

"So, you have seen the woman?" It was not a question.

"Yes, Great One. You have taken excellent care of her. The duke will be delighted."

"Will he now? And he is the duke of…?"

"Richmond." It was a safe choice. Tristan was certain Moulay was not so familiar with the peerage that he would question this.

Moulay nodded thoughtfully, pursing his lips, and Tristan tensed. The sultan was not a stupid man. He clapped his hands and Tristan nearly jumped out of his skin. But Moulay was only ordering refreshments. Perhaps this was to be uncomplicated after all. An exchange of treasure and a promise of alliance and Tristan and Olivia would be sailing home. Calm washed over him and the tension in his neck eased.

Several servants arrived with trays of salads which were placed before the two. Dried fruit and olives and flatbread came next. There were empty cups and a vessel that appeared to be a teapot. Then came platters of meat, the smells mouth-watering. Tristan realized he hadn't eaten much in the past few days and the fare looked wonderful.

A servant stepped forward and picked up the teapot. Holding the pitcher well above the table, he poured. Hot steaming liquid, ripe with the odor of mint, filled the air and flowed down into the waiting cups. The tea formed bubbles and the sultan nodded his approval. The man picked up his cup and drank, then nodded to Tristan to do the same. The drink was soothing and delicious. Following the sultan's lead, he ate with his fingers and used the flatbread to soak up the juices. It was barbaric but strangely satisfying.

Finally, the sultan leaned back and belched, patting his stomach.

"So now we can speak about the arrangements."

"I am prepared, Great One. How shall we make the exchange?" Tristan leaned forward expectantly.

"I will send some of my soldiers to your ship to retrieve my treasure. Then we can negotiate the alliance."

"Of course, Great One. But, forgive me for my suggesting otherwise, but would it be possible to finalize our agreements first so we can be on our way? The duke would not like to miss the birth of his son and heir."

"And this duke is convinced she carries a male?"

Tristan smiled. "Of course."

"Women lie, you know." The sultan looked him directly in the eye, but Tristan didn't flinch.

"I suppose some do, Great One. But my lady has no reason to do so. The duke wishes her back no matter what the child's gender. He has made that clear."

Moulay sucked in his cheeks. His eyes narrowed and his lips flattened. "I am certain a week or so will make little difference. From what I have been told, the woman is barely showing." Moulay lifted an eyebrow. "Or perhaps you think to abscond with my treasure and not hold up your end of the bargain?"

"I would never presume to be so foolish as to try outsmarting you, Great One." Tristan bowed his head to emphasize his words.

"Good, good." But Moulay did not sound convinced. "Did you bring papers from your king to assure me of the intent of the alliance?"

"Of course, but they are in my rooms." Before Tristan could say more, the sultan clapped his hands again and two guards immediately stepped forward. Moulay motioned one of the men to lean down and then whispered in his ear. The soldier straightened and the two strode from the room.

"I am certain you would not mind that I sent them to retrieve the documents. I have no doubt your escorts will willingly give them to my guards." Moulay raised an eyebrow, as if daring Tristan to disagree.

"Of course, Great One." He stood to follow the soldiers, but Moulay waved him back down.

"Oh, no. Sit, relax after your meal. You must let it digest." His forced grin suggested he was victorious and Tristan's inside roiled with fury. If they gave up all they had too soon, they would have no more to bargain. He wanted to be aboard the ship before all was handed over. If anyone was able to discern the documents were not genuine, they would all die. Tristan had hoped to delay the sultan's men by going with them and stalling, and he wondered if Felix and Leo would hand over the papers or resist. Either way did not bode well since Tristan feared losing any advantage. The more time the sultan had to examine the treaty, the greater the risk.

He counseled himself to relax. Moulay had no experts to check the legitimacy of the contract supposedly from the king. Believing the papers to be real, the sultan had to know no bargain would be struck if he did not uphold his side and release Olivia. Let him have the papers. They looked genuine and would not betray their true origin. Catherine had done a masterful job. If Tristan hadn't known better, he would swear they had been signed by the king himself.

*** 

Early the next morning, Sabra appeared at Olivia's door. She looked both ways down the corridor, then scurried over to Olivia's cot and sat on the edge. Olivia had just awakened and was puzzled at seeing her visitor.

Sabra leaned in. "Is it true?" She sounded breathless with excitement.

Olivia was still held in the arms of sleep and her thinking was muddled. "Is what true?"

"You carry a child? An English nobleman's child?" Sabra's eyes widened with her hunger for an answer.

Olivia's initial instinct was to say no, of course not. She was a virgin. But her mind cleared, and she was amazed word had traveled without delay. Braheem warned there were no secrets in the harem. That Sabra had heard of her *condition* so quickly confirmed that.

"Yes, yes, it is true." She hoped she sounded convincing.

"Your friend says it is a lie." An eyebrow eased up.

Sabra must have meant Amelia. "She does not know. I did not feel the need to confide in her."

Sabra narrowed her eyes and angled her head. "But were you not aboard the same ship for weeks? How could she not have suspected?"

81

"These clothes conceal much, Sabra. And I am not so far along that my belly protrudes overmuch."

Sabra dropped her gaze, then smiled. "You know I am your friend, yes?"

"Why would I doubt that?" The lie slid easily from her tongue. Olivia wondered where this conversation was going. "Is there someone who is not my friend?"

Sabra dropped her gaze again. "I would not trust Maha. She tells untruths." This was spoken in a whisper.

"Odd, that you tell me this. Maha does not speak your language, so how would you know what she says?" Olivia tried to keep accusation from her tone, but she knew she failed.

Sabra stood and straightened her spine. "I was just trying to warn you. You had best be careful, lest the others feel the need to show their dislike."

A quote Olivia had read from "The Prince" by Machiavelli, came into her head. *Keep your friends close and your enemies closer.* She reached out her hand.

"Forgive me, Sabra. I had no intention to offend you. I have no doubt your motives are pure. I think the changes in my body have set my nerves on edge."

Sabra reluctantly nodded and eased back down. "I was just showing concern." Her bottom lip stuck out in an unnatural pout.

If the hair on Olivia's nape had not tightened, she might believe this woman. But every instinct told her not to trust Sabra. She must remember to watch every word. And glean as much information as possible.

"How did you know?" Olivia prodded. "I still do not believe I show so very much."

Sabra tilted her head, her half-smile reflecting her pleasure. "I have my ways of finding information."

"Will you share?" Olivia tried to sound deferential and pleading at the same time.

"Of course," Sabra smiled again, but it didn't reach her eyes. "The eunuchs go between the harem and the palace. There are no secrets if one knows who to befriend." She leaned in closer. "Some are friendlier than others, if you know the right inducement."

Olivia tried to hide her shock at this. "You mean... seduction?"

Sabra glared at Olivia as if she had lost her wits. "Of course not. The eunuchs have nothing to... Do you not understand the nature of a eunuch?"

Olivia cheeks heated with her blush. "I do."

Sabra shook her head in dismissal. "But there are favors one can offer."

"Like?" Olivia prodded.

Sabra heaved a sigh, clearly deciding how much she should reveal. "Coin, jewels, sometimes even potions." Sabra licked her lips.

"Potions?"

Sabra shook her head in disgust. "Do you know nothing? A potion can do so many things, depending on its ingredients."

Now Olivia was shaken, but she dared not show it to this woman. Sabra was talking about poisons. Were they so easily accessible here?

"Would one of the guards poison the women?" Olivia widened her eyes.

Sabra laughed without mirth. "They would sooner use it on each other. How else could one rise so easily in the ranks?" She lifted her chin. "So, if I were you, I would be cautious."

"Me? But why?" A shiver ran up Olivia's spine at the change in topic.

"I think you might have enemies here."

There was a note of triumph in her tone that made Olivia very uneasy. Enemies? Of course. She had arrived with Amelia and Charlotte and Charlotte had already been chosen ahead of the others. Then Olivia, too, would be viewed as competition. And Amelia. Could the woman really blame her for Charlotte's death? Olivia inhaled and blew out the breath. Yes, Sabra was right. Olivia needed to take every precaution to ensure her safety. She might, in her condition, be safe from the sultan, but that did not mean she was safe.

Sabra leaned in closer. "I will confide in you my secret. That way you will know I am sincere."

"Secret?" Olivia was very curious.

"I am to advance in my training. The sultan will soon send for me."

"That is good news," Olivia responded. "When will this happen?"

"Soon. There is one small impediment, but it will go away very soon. So, I thought you might want to know so you can be my friend. I can offer much as soon as the sultan has declared me one of his favorites." She sat back in a satisfied posture.

"That is very kind of you. I am pleased." Every hair on Olivia's nape was standing now. Instinct told her Sabra was a woman who gave nothing unless she was rewarded tenfold.

"Of course, friends help each other." Sabra flicked her wrist as if it was a very offhand remark.

Now, Olivia's suspicions were confirmed. "Of course I will help you. Any way I can."

"Good. I will let you know when I require proof of your loyalty." And she slipped form the room. Olivia had no idea what Sabra would ask of her, but she was certain she wouldn't like it.

# Chapter Five

Tristan returned to his apartments, but neither Felix nor Leo were in evidence. His first thought was they had been taken. He took a deep breath and logic prevailed. There would be no reason for the sultan to order that. He quickly moved to the mattress and lifted it. Undisturbed, the documents Catherine had so expertly forged remained untouched. But what if his men had been detained because they could not produce the papers? Tristan had not revealed where he had hidden them. No, that would not make sense.

Tristan sank onto the bed and considered all his options. He had two men and a crew on a ship in the distant harbor. Certainly not enough to attack or even defend. Olivia was sequestered away in another part of the palace grounds, no doubt heavily guarded. Clenching his teeth together, he worked his jaw in frustration. He had been convinced he had gained headway with Moulay, but his missing men made him apprehensive.

Just as he was considering ways he could get some leverage, the brothers entered the apartments.

"Where have you been?" Tristan jumped to his feet, his relief coming to the fore in his tone. Tristan witnessed what Moulay could do and these men were his loyal friends.

"We decided to discover what we could about the design of this place." Felix leaned in and lowered his voice. "It is always good to have a route out, do you not agree?" Felix explained. "Not that the sultan is untrustworthy." His sarcasm oozed.

"I do agree. I have been exploring at night, as well. Have you found anything of interest?"

"No," said Leo. "But we shall not give up. But we were also concerned for your safety. You were gone quite a while. Did you meet with the sultan?"

"Yes. He demanded the treaty documents and sent his soldiers to retrieve them. Did you not encounter them?"

Leo shook his head. "No doubt we had already left these rooms when they came to collect them."

Tristan nodded with relief. "Good. A little delay should work in our favor. And yes, exploring our options…that was a wise move. And were you unmolested?"

"The soldiers barely glanced our way. Either they have been instructed to leave us alone or they think of us as no threat," Leo said, shrugging.

"I prefer to believe they are too afraid of retribution if they cross us. We are very intimidating." This from Felix who stood straighter to emphasize his comment. Leo nodded his agreement.

"Tell me everything you saw." Tristan encouraged, ignoring the last comment.

"Naught encouraging. There are guards everywhere. The only possibility for escape would be to find a way to distract them," Leo said, shaking his head.

"Then we will do just that. As soon as we have Olivia in our grasp," Tristan affirmed.

"And how do you plan to do that?" Leo asked.

Tristan really didn't know. They needed to find the best escape route should they not be allowed to leave on their own. John and Catherine had given him a rough layout of both the palace and the harem, but none of the possibilities seemed to guarantee their safe passage back to their ship.

Tristan shrugged. "I was hoping you both would help me figure that out."

\*\*\*

Olivia blinked awake and let her thoughts clear. Sunlight dappled the mosaics covering the walls and floor, painting them with gold. It was beautiful here and if she had been a guest under other circumstances, she might have appreciated the incredible intricacy and loveliness of her surroundings. As it was, her only thought was that she could not wait to leave this place behind. She wondered how much time it would take for the "ambassador" to secure her release. If the sultan believed her with an English noble's child, they would not dare wait too long. The idea comforted.

She got up and dressed and made her way down the corridor to the open area with the fountains. Even at this early hour, it was crowded with women. As she entered the space, she felt a different atmosphere. It was still an adjustment to see so many with so little clothing, but some of the women actually nodded to her in greeting. It occurred to her she was the one who was the oddity, fully dressed as she was. But this morning, the women did not turn their backs on her and one or two actually smiled. Olivia mentally shrugged. She would not be here long, and she had prepared herself to manage the isolation until it was time to go. Now, though, the women seemed almost welcoming.

"Good morning. I trust you slept well," said one woman in Arabic, stepping over to her. "I am Ra'naa. It means 'one to gaze at'." We all like to know what our new names mean. I am not certain why, except it makes them easier to accept, I suppose." The woman was very pretty, with dark eyes and long black hair that curled around her head. Her skin was a lovely shade of dark chocolate.

"I am Daizi. It means 'light'." This woman was also beautiful, but her skin was a pale pink and her hair light brown. "Please join us for some food." The woman took Olivia's hand and led her over to the tables groaning with delectables.

She found herself looking for Maha, but the other woman was nowhere in sight. Her stomach growled and she realized she was starving. If she ate heartily in front of the others, it would reinforce the idea that she was eating for two. Suddenly, the change in the women's attitudes made sense. That was why these women were suddenly so welcoming. If she was with child and the babe was not the sultan's, she was no longer a threat. And, with such limited exposure to the outside world, they must be anxious for new conversation.

The women were now chattering away among themselves, so Olivia picked up a bowl and was perusing the offerings when she was shoved from behind. The crockery flew into the air as she was thrown forward. She slammed into something unyielding, pain exploded in her head, and she fell forward. The bowl crashed and splintered into pieces, just missing her head. She was vaguely aware of a few gasps and the cold tiles underneath her cheek before she was sucked down into the blackness.

The next thought was her head pounding as though it had been hit with a heavy object. Memory eased back. She had struck her head on the corner of the table. Someone had pushed her. She blinked and it took her a moment to realize she was laying on her bed, now, and the pain was relentless. Reaching up to the throbbing spot, something sticky clung to her fingers. She looked at them and saw blood.

"It looks worse than it is." The soft, familiar voice was as soothing as the cool cloth placed upon her forehead. Maha smiled down at her.

Olivia smiled back. "You must think me very clumsy."

"I think you were attacked from behind," she replied, anger edging her tone.

"Attacked? By whom? And why?"

Maha shrugged. "No one actually saw who did it, but it was obvious. You flew forward too quickly to have merely slipped."

"Yes, I was shoved, but I have no idea why." Olivia did not want to believe anyone in the harem would deliberately try to harm her. Why just this morning, they had been so kind to her. It made no sense. Unless…

"Yes." It was as if the other woman read her thoughts. "I have no doubt it was your so-called friend. No one else would bother with you." Maha's hand flew to her mouth. "I mean no insult."

"No insult taken." Olivia managed a weak smile.

"It's just that the other women would not waste time worrying over another's misfortune. You are just something new and different to them. They might be kinder to you, but their true interests lie in competing for the sultan's favor." Maha shook her head. "Does Amelia truly believe you had anything to do with the death of her sister?"

Olivia nodded. "I don't know. I think she needs someone to blame. But, I do not know any way to convince her otherwise. All of this," she waved her hand around the area, trying not to make any sudden movements, "has been too much for her, I think."

"Her mind has become unhinged?" Maha sounded very concerned.

"I fear so." Despair for Amelia pulled at Olivia's heart.

"You must not let her near you again. I will speak to Jaffar. He is the head eunuch. He will see her controlled."

"Oh, no. I do not wish her punished," Olivia replied, aghast at Amelia suffering even more. She could not be angry at Amelia. She knew how she felt when Catherine was taken from them years ago. Olivia was full of rage and would have liked someone close by to blame .

Maha smiled. "She will not be punished," the other woman assured her. "But she will be watched more closely. Amelia is a danger. If she attacks you, she could go after anyone. It cannot be tolerated."

Olivia smiled at Maha. "Thank you for taking care of me. I am fine, now." A thought struck. "Where have you been? I was looking for you this morning."

Maha swallowed visibly. "I am but a reed in the wind. I must go whenever any of the others need tending. And, it was decided I should come and care for you." Maha leaned in conspiratorially. "The truth is, I wished to speak to you alone anyway. I have heard you carry a nobleman's child and are soon to be sent back to England."

"Yes." Olivia tried to keep her tone without emotion. *Everyone has heard.*

"But when you woke up just now, you did not ask as to the welfare of the babe." Maha's tone was flat, expectant.

"Oh, I…" Olivia did not know what to say. Maha was right. An expectant mother would be more concerned for her child's health than her own after such a trauma.

"It matters not. I must assume you have a reason for your deceit." She looked Olivia directly in the eye. "I will tell no one, on one condition. You must take me with you." When Olivia did not respond immediately, Maha clasped her hands together, "I beg you." A tear coursed down Maha's cheek. "I cannot bear it here."

Reaching out her hand, Olivia patted the other woman's arm. "How long…"

"Have I been here? Two years, give or take. It seems like ten."

"Tell me how you came to be here in the beginning," Olivia encouraged. She wondered if Maha had been kidnapped as well.

Maha dropped her chin. "My father sent me away." Her voice trembled as she spoke the words, but she did not cry more.

Olivia gasped. "What? Your father sold you to the sultan?" She couldn't believe she had heard Maha correctly. Of course, her sister-in-law's unscrupulous relatives had done much the same to Shera. It was unspeakable.

"No, not directly. My mother died when I was born, and my father's new wife did not want me around. Especially after I…walked in on her…" Her voice broke.

"With another man?" Olivia questioned softly.

"With my brother." She dropped her gaze to the floor.

Olivia's stomach turned over at the thought. "Oh no. That is terrible. Does your father know?"

Maha shrugged. "He would not believe me. The woman has him totally besotted."

"I am so sorry."

"So, she made up some lies about my mistreatment of her. Of *her*! And my father sent me to an English cousin. I suppose he had no way of knowing the man was a disgusting lecher. Of course, he was English and that alone was terrible enough." She pressed her lips together and tears filled her eyes. "Forgive me, my lady. I did not mean to say…about the English."

Olivia grinned. "I am aware of the Scottish enmity for your English neighbors. I am not offended. Go on with your story," Olivia prodded.

Maha nodded, her expression one of gratitude. "I try to believe my father sent me to our relative thinking I might have a better life." Maha inhaled slowly and shrugged. "I hope that was his reasoning. No matter now." She inhaled again, choking back a sob. "My cousin tried to…abuse me one night and I managed to get away. I ran as far and as fast as I could, and ended up at the wharf, right into the arms of a kidnapper. And so here I am."

Olivia pressed a hand to her chest. The poor woman had been dealt such an unfair hand in life. "Oh, Maha, no one deserves what you have suffered."

Maha shrugged. "It got worse. I have red hair and that is not valued here, so I became an Odalisque, a servant. Some of the women still fear I carry a curse, but most have come to accept me. Others, however, feel it is acceptable to take out their frustrations on me." Maha pivoted and lowered her garments from her shoulders. Scars threaded ugly patterns across the flesh of her back. Olivia's heart broke for the other woman. No one should have to bear such abuse, especially not one as kind as

Maha. She covered herself and turned back around. "And I am to be at the pleasure of any man, *any man*, who desires to have a woman. Which means the sultan has no use for me for himself. Even if I could tolerate his attentions, I will never have the chance to rise in rank. So you see, I hate it here." This last was whispered and her gaze lowered.

Sadness threatened to pull Olivia into its unyielding darkness. As terrible as her own situation was, at least she had a loving family who cared for her. To be so abandoned and mistreated was unthinkable. "My sister-in-law, Shera, has red hair. The others here feared her, too."

"Here? Your sister-in-law was here? She is no longer? Did she…" Maha stammered, not able to form the words.

Olivia smiled reassuringly and shook her head. "She is not dead. My brother helped her escape and they are now in England and married with two beautiful children." Olivia prayed that they were indeed well and Nabil had not done them harm. She recalled Tristan's covert reassurance and the fear dissipated.

"She escaped?" Maha's eyes widened. "How?"

"Actually, my brother helped her. First, he was responsible for her kidnapping, and then he helped her to freedom." Olivia knew this must be confusing.

"You see, my sister, Catherine, was here also. She had been taken first and my brother wished Shera's aid in arranging for Catherine's escape. It turned out Catherine was in love and had no wish to leave. Until she was betrayed by a very evil man, who had her lover arrested and forced Catherine to marry him instead."

Maha scooted closer, fascinated. "What happened to your sister?"

"She managed an escape and found her way home."

"Then there is hope?" Maha was nearly breathless with excitement.

"There is always hope." Olivia prayed her belief would prove true.

"So you will take me with you?" Maha's tone was pleading and Olivia did not have the heart to deny her. "I could work for you and your family. I would cause no trouble."

What choice did she have. She could not leave Maha here. The woman had suffered enough. "I will take you with us when we go."

"Do you promise?"

"I promise." Olivia feared she might regret this vow, but she had no choice. She could not bear to leave her new friend behind, not wishing Maha to suffer more.

***

Tristan and his men waited as afternoon passed into night. No one came to their apartments except servants bringing food. No more soldiers appeared demanding documents and that fact put Tristan on edge. The sultan was playing a game and Tristan could not figure out what it was. But he was certain it was a deadly exercise that threatened them all.

There was nothing to do but wait upon the pleasure of Moulay and Tristan's nerves were growing tighter by the minute. He tried to sleep, but it escaped him. His thoughts were filled by his beautiful Olivia and his fervent desire to release her from the sultan's dangerous control. He was helpless and he hated the feeling.

The following morning, two soldiers appeared at Tristan's apartments, flanking Leo and Felix. One of the guards angled his head, indicating Tristan was to join them. Tristan nodded, hoping against hope they would be taking them to Olivia.

Down corridors and across a courtyard, this time mercifully empty of men waiting on the sultan's mood. Tristan could see what had to be the building that housed the harem. It was down a cobbled pathway but may as well have been a thousand miles away. He longed to rush into the structure and capture Olivia. That would be foolish and futile. They would never make it to the ship. Why, he was certain to be cut down before he could so much as breach the threshold.

Tristan and the others continued on their way, through another entrance to the palace and then down more labyrinthine halls and finally were led into a large room. Again, pillows filled the corners and were gathered around tables.

The soldiers gestured for them to sit while servants bustled in with trays of food. Tristan wondered if these people did anything other than eat. Or, in the sultan's case, amuse himself by procreating or taking the lives of others.

Once seated, with plates of exotic edibles in front of them, they were surprised by six women entering the space. Their faces were obscured with veils, but Tristan knew instantly that Olivia was not among them. Disappointment pulled at him.

One of the women, who had a shock of red hair, stationed herself against the wall near the guards, while two of the other women took up instruments and sat down to play. The other three danced to the increasingly faster music, their hips gyrating and their hands and arms twisting into impossible shapes. Leo and Felix were riveted, their eyes wide. Tristan leaned over to Felix.

"And what is your wife's name, again?"

Felix dropped his head, then gave Tristan a sidelong glance. "Truly, I am married, and I care for my wife, but I have not yet been consigned to a grave. I cannot help but appreciate a beautiful woman—or several."

Leo, however, was paying little attention to the entertainment. He appeared transfixed by the red-haired woman standing apart from the others, next to the guards.

"Is she a servant?" he inquired to no one in particular.

Before either of his companions could respond, the woman scooted forward and made her way to the men's table. She reached for a teapot and poured the pungent mint liquid into each man's cup. Then, she scurried away and pressed herself back against the wall.

"She is breathtaking," Leo said. He smiled and, catching her eye, she lowered her gaze, but not before he could see the color rising above the veil and flushing her cheeks. "Dare we inquire who she is?"

Tristan peered over in disgust. "Leo, we are here to save Olivia, not see your fantasies fulfilled. Remember your mission."

Clearly embarrassed, Leo nodded. "But, if it were possible, perhaps we could rescue another?" This was a whisper.

"Love at first sight, brother?" Felix teased. "Or lust?"

Leo heaved a sigh. "I cannot imagine any of these women are happy here. Although, I suppose the favorites have found contentment. But that girl has fire in her green eyes. A fire for freedom."

Tristan notice the look in Leo's eyes. He wasn't looking upon the woman with lewd ideas. It was more an infatuation. "And so now you read minds?" Tristan lifted an eyebrow.

Leo shrugged. "You do not have to read minds to know.

"No," Tristan agreed. But the thought of adding another when their own odds of escape were ever diminishing was disheartening.

The music wound down and the women surrounded them, touching their faces and stroking their arms seductively. Tristan was not fooled. This was another test by the sultan, but Tristan was unsure as to what the ruler expected.

The three dancers sidled over closer. Each chose one of the men and the music began again. Up close, it was obvious the women were clothed only in silken scarves. As the music wrapped around the room, the women unwrapped their garments. Only their long tresses concealed their bare breasts and a bit of fabric covered their most intimate parts. Their hips swayed seductively as they wound their bodies around the men, teasing, touching.

Tristan groaned as his body reacted to the temptation. Almond-shaped eyes and taut breasts beckoned. A scarf wrapped around his neck and seductively pulled. The women smelled of exotic scents he could not name. Maybe in another time, under different circumstances, he would partake of what was offered, But, not only was his heart with Olivia, he was also keenly aware this was but a diversion, a trick to sway them from their duties.

The women continued their siren's movements, knowing they were getting a physical response from their audience. But, finally, when none the men surrendered, they gave up and, clearly frustrated, grabbed the bits of clothing they had dropped and stormed from the room.

"Whew," Felix exclaimed. "Both of you must remember to tell my wife what a good husband I am."

"Remarkable," Tristan breathed. "And I must love Olivia even more than I imagined." He glanced at Leo, who appeared transfixed by the woman with red hair still hugging the far wall. "And what if she were one of the dancers?" he asked.

"Then I would have retired to another room for more privacy. Perhaps I can manage to be alone with her anyway. What think you?" He could not hide the smile that lit his eyes.

The woman smiled at Leo and Tristan had to wonder if she understood Leo's comments. But Tristan saw no reason to object to an hour or two of respite for his man. Tristan nodded and Leo stood and moved to her, then looked to the soldiers for approval. One of them bowed acquiescence and indicated a nook off to the side. Leo looked over his shoulder at his companions and grinned wider. Then, Leo took her hand and she willingly followed.

The soldiers strode forward and indicated the other men were to come with them. They led Tristan and Felix back to their apartments and disappeared. If this had been a test by the sultan, Tristan wondered if they had passed or failed.

\*\*\*

Olivia's head still throbbed slightly, but she had otherwise recovered from her fall. Maha had been gone all the next day, apparently to tend her other duties. Olivia missed the companionship. She stretched and realized she was starving. Dizziness held her in place for a moment until the room righted. Slowly rising from her bed, Olivia made her way to the main room. Cautiously looking around to make sure no one was near enough to threaten her, she filled a plate with food and strode to one of the benches to eat. Again, several of the women greeted her. One approached her meekly. "I am Amena. I am sorry for your…accident. I am happy you have recovered." Her words seemed sincere.

"Thank you. I am quite well now."

"And the babe. It was unharmed by your fall?" The concern in her tone was clear.

Olivia took the hint and rubbed her hand over her stomach. "I am convinced the babe is fine. It was only my head that was damaged. I thank you for asking." So, she was no longer considered a threat to the others since they believed she carried a child that did not come from the sultan.

Before the other woman could say more, a movement on the other side of the room caught Olivia's eye. Braheem tilted his head to indicate she should meet him in the corridor behind him.

"If you will forgive me, I am suddenly feeling a little ill." Olivia stood, hoping the other woman would think she had morning sickness and walk away. Amena stroked Olivia's arm in sympathy and stood also, then disappeared among the other women.

Olivia took her empty plate back to the table, nonchalantly glanced about. No one was watching, so she eased her way over to the place he had designated. It was dark and she had to move slowly, feeling her way.

She nearly jumped out of her skin when he appeared in front of her. "Braheem? What is it? Is something amiss?"

"I bring news, but I am unsure if it is good or bad."

It was too dark to read his expression, but Olivia tensed at his words. "Tell me," she whispered.

"The sultan is toying with your ambassador and his escorts. He sent women to seduce them. Only one of the men accepted the invitation."

Olivia pressed her lips together and her muscles tensed. "Which one?" Olivia swallowed her apprehension. Was Tristan the man who accepted?

He took a deep breath and blew it out. "I know not. Except the sultan does not like his offers to be refused. He will not be pleased that they did not all succumb to the charms of his women."

Olivia gasped. "Will he try to hurt the ambassador or his men?" Moulay's temper was legendary and a shiver ran up her spine imagining his retribution if he were insulted.

"Oh, I doubt that. They still carry the weight of the English crown and I think he would not dare risk offending your king in such a way."

Olivia exhaled a sigh of relief.

"There is more."

Olivia bit her lower lip. "Go on."

"The woman you came with…"

"Amelia."

"Yes, Amelia, has requested an audience with the sultan. She asked Jaffar to intercede for her. I can only imagine she intends to malign you. She spews her hate for you to whoever will listen. Luckily, most do not understand her words."

Olivia pondered this for a moment. "Will the sultan see her? And, will he believe her?" She was both nervous and angry now and her voice shook. She had done naught but show kindness to the other woman, but Amelia had it out for her.

"The sultan will not grant her wish since she is not a

favorite. He does not accede to the desires of females unless it suits him. However, Jaffar might take it upon himself to carry the woman's words, and then the sultan will do what he does. Moulay is a very unpredictable man. The only sure thing is that he will slice off a head at his whim. He might give her message credibility, or he might demand the end of her life. There is no telling."

"So we must wait?"

"Unfortunately, yes. But I am working on a strategy that might prove beneficial to you and your ambassador."

"Can you tell me?" Hope suffused her.

"I can tell you this. There are secret passageways out of the harem, but once outside, finding sanctuary is most difficult. But, if that does not have merit, another idea will come. Do not worry. I will protect you."

"Braheem, you risk so much for me. Why?"

He leaned in. "The sultan has cost me much. I would like to see him lose something he values." He bowed and he disappeared down the corridor. Olivia thought there were things she knew naught of, but was delighted Braheem was willing to offer her aid.

Secret passageways. That was an intriguing thought. If only she could manage to communicate to Tristan, perhaps it would help. Olivia slipped back into the main room and sat on the edge of one of the fountains. She trailed her hand in the warm water, thoughts swirling in her head. Braheem had promised again to protect her and she knew he meant his words. But how much could he do against the sultan. And was he sufficiently connected to find them an escape route?

Olivia glanced over at the far wall. Amelia was sitting on one of the benches, pounding her fists against the sides of her head. She rocked back and forth, her mouth moving, but no sound emerged. Olivia dearly wished she could reason with the other woman, but it was too late for that. It was clear her mind was shattered.

Nearby, a very large man hovered, watching Amelia's every move. This must be Jaffar, the head eunuch. It was no wonder he was in charge. The man was huge and powerfully built. Who would dare challenge him? His height was well over seven feet and his chest and shoulders were as broad as those of two men put together. He appeared transfixed by Amelia who barely seemed to notice him.

After a few minutes, he prepared a plate of food and brought it to her. He knelt in front of her and offered up the delicacies. She gave him a wan smile and picked at some fruit. He rose and stepped away, but he kept his eyes on her. Olivia decided he was probably just making certain she threatened no one else. But still, his behavior toward Amelia seemed out of place.

Her thoughts drifted to Tristan. Had he slept with another? Had he tired of trying to free her and decided to give in to temptation? No, he would not betray her in such a manner. He had come for her, risking all. But she wanted to see him, to look into his eyes and know he loved only her. Unknowing was a torment. She ached for the comfort of his arms.

Olivia pulled her gaze back to the ripples in the pool and thought how one action affected so many other things. Powerlessness threatened to steal her hope and resolve, and she fought the feeling back. As long as she breathed, there was a chance to find a way home.

# Chapter Six

Two more miserable days had dragged past. Finally, the sultan had asked for another audience. Tristan was escorted alone this time and took his place at the feet of Moulay.

"I must ask you again the name of the nobleman who has laid claim to the female."

Suspicion swirled. "The Duke of Richmond." Tristan knew if he elaborated, it would sound suspect.

The sultan pulled at his beard. "Where is my treasure?"

"Forgive me, Great One. I have not had the opportunity to collect it. It remains aboard my ship, and quite safe."

"I want it now." His tone was flat, without any intonation. Just an order that defied disagreement.

"Then I shall send for it immediately." Tristan wanted to hold out as long as possible, preferring to get Olivia onboard before giving up any of his leverage.

"No! You shall remain here. Send word it is to be brought to me." The sultan's eyes narrowed, and the threat was clear.

"Great One, I would not be so foolish as to trust the location of such riches with any of my men. It is well-concealed and safe, but only I know where. I could not risk having it taken from you yet again." He studied the sultan's expression, but it remained neutral. The man was an enigma and therefore all the more dangerous.

"But can we not conduct all of our business at the same time?" he continued. "I shall gladly give you what rightfully belongs to you as well as the treaty, but I do wish to be on my way with the lady. Surely you can understand, in her delicate state, she should be allowed to go home as soon as possible."

"Why should I believe you? Since I have been informed that the Duke of Richmond cannot possibly have fathered this so-called heir."

Tristan was shocked. Why would he say such a thing? The sultan cannot know so much of the English peerage. Someone must have given him information and Tristan needed to assure that the sultan accepted his veracity over that of the talebearer. Or, the man was bluffing to test Tristan's reaction. He needed to stand his ground.

"Ah, Great One. But I can assure you the nobleman in question has fathered this child. Perhaps you have heard something other than the truth, since the Duke prefers to opt for discretion. After all, he is married." Tristan gave the sultan a conspiratorial smile.

The sultan pondered this for a moment and appeared satisfied, but Tristan could not be certain. He could see the man working through the risks of making the wrong choices. Moulay was a god in this country, but he could certainly not withstand an assault from England. Especially over a female.

Finally, after what seemed hours, but was actually only minutes, the sultan nodded. He lifted his hands in the air and clapped them together twice. Two soldiers hastened over.

"I believe I must have the woman examined. Will that tell a different tale?" The sultan was surely challenging him now. Did he mean to examine Olivia or was he referring to another who had spoken words against her? Or was he just testing the waters to gauge Tristan's reaction?

Tristan's stomach clenched. Would he dare try Olivia seen by a physician to determine if she was indeed with child? If so, they would be doomed. But then, what else could it be? Who would go against him and Olivia? It made no sense. But, now was not the time to panic. He must stand firm and convince the sultan to believe him. This was a game of cat-and-mouse and Tristan had no intention of becoming the mouse. Their lives depended on it.

\*\*\*

Maha came fluttering into Olivia's room. Her cheeks were flushed with excitement.

"My lady, my lady, I have a question. I must know."

Olivia eyed her quizzically. "All right. What is it?"

"The ambassador. Or rather the men with him."

Olivia was puzzled. "I have no knowledge who is with him, but I would guess I know them not." Olivia knew whoever came with Tristan must be men the sultan would not recognize. "What of them?"

"Not them. Him."

"Who?" Olivia had no idea who Maha was talking about. Was something amiss with one of Tristan's escorts? Her apprehension eased when she realized Maha was grinning. In fact, Maha was barely containing her excitement. She was shifting from one foot to another.

"The man with the ambassador." Maha clasped her hands in front to emphasize her frustration.

"I do not know who you mean. What man?" Her tone was calm, hoping to settle the other woman enough to get some clarity.

Maha took a deep breath. "The ambassador has an escort of two men. They are both very appealing, but the one is…" She sounded as if she were about to swoon. "He is called Leo."

Olivia tilted her head. "Leo, is he? Like a lion?"

"Oh, no. He has a kind look, the look of a man who treats a woman well." She closed her eyes in memory. "And, in fact, he is a wonderful man."

"I see. And you know all this because you have seen him but once?" Olivia tried to mask her skepticism.

"No, no, I spent the afternoon with him yesterday. I would have come to you sooner, but I was kept busy with so many chores. The other women, the dancers, wished to punish me for being the one chosen."

Relief flowed through Olivia as she realized Leo had been the man to choose a woman, not Tristan. Not that she had doubted the man she loved.

"I take it your encounter with him was a pleasant interlude." Olivia grinned suggestively.

"I want him to marry me." She sighed. "As soon as we escape, that is."

"Oh, that is all we have to accomplish? To escape the inescapable?" Olivia shook her head.

"My lady, there is always a way. As you told me, you merely have to have faith."

Olivia jumped up at this. "You know something? Some way to get out of the harem and find our way to freedom?"

Maha took a step back and dropped her head. "Not exactly. But it has been done before. You said so yourself."

"Yes, but both times, the woman had help from the outside. We have no such aid, except the ambassador. We must pray for his success." And Olivia did pray, with every fiber of her being, that Tristan would somehow manage to convince Moulay to let them go.

Maha's chin lifted. "I have faith. The way Leo looked at me, I know he will secure our freedom. With the help of the ambassador, of course." Maha tilted her head. "I know you have no reason to trust me, my lady, but then, you have no reason not to. I will do everything I can to help."

Olivia knew in her heart Maha spoke the truth. Olivia had often been accused of snap judgments in the past, but so far, her instincts had not failed. She had chosen her horse from a stable of many after one glance and he had proven himself time and time again. She had recognized Tristan as her true love the moment she saw him. And that same intuition told her she could rely on this woman.

"Braheem is someone you can confide in," Olivia whispered.

Maha smiled. "I always liked him best among our guards. He seems to pale whenever the sultan or one of the wives does something cruel. I know he does not approve of so much that happens here."

Worry creased Olivia's brow. "Has anyone else noticed these reactions of his?"

Maha shook her head. "I doubt it. Most of the other women are much too concerned with their beauty or their comfort. Or elevating their station here if they are not among the chosen. Looking into the face of a eunuch would have no interest for them."

"And what thoughts occupy your mind?" Olivia asked gently. "What has kept you sane in your time as a captive here? How have you not fallen into despair?"

"Aside from hoping for escape? It was the belief that I would find a good man to love me. Like Leo. And if we have children, I will never turn them out." The raw pain on her face was heartbreaking.

*** 

The waiting was interminable, and Tristan knew he was losing the advantage. He had to do something to force the sultan's hand without putting them all at risk. But he was in a quandary, since he had no idea what was happening with Olivia. And, knowing the unpredictable moods of Moulay, he dare not push too far. Perhaps he should just present the treasure and the forged parchments from the king and hope the sultan would be honorable. Of course, that was like expecting a scorpion to be morally upright.

Leo strode into Tristan's apartment, the grin on his face telling.

"Did you enjoy your time?" Tristan asked, raising an eyebrow.

"Ah, ye of little faith. I have discovered much. Of course, I did not suffer in the discovery, but what matters that?"

Felix appeared behind his brother. He gave Leo a playful shove, then glared at him. "Well?"

Leo looked about to ensure no one listened. "The harem is heavily guarded."

Tristan shook his head. "Tell us something we don't know." Sarcasm coated his words.

"What you don't know is that the guards concern themselves mostly with the favorites. There is a definite hierarchy. There is first and foremost the Valide Sultan. She is the most powerful and can even intercede with the sultan if the ministers think he has made an erroneous decision. Or, if she simply has a mind to exact some punishment or change. Then come the four Kadins, who are the sultan's favorites. These women change as the sultan tires of them or they no longer can bear children. Heavens above, the man is said to have fathered over nine-hundred." Leo crossed his hands over his heart. He was clearly impressed by this.

"Go on," Tristan encouraged.

"These chosen women have their own servants. And, on the very bottom are the Odalisques. They serve anyone and everyone above them. The eunuchs pay very little attention to these women, since they have no real value. They are merely slaves." And he grinned. "And Maha, the woman I chose, is an Odalisque."

Tristan rubbed his chin in understanding. "Which means she has more freedom than many." He nodded his head approvingly. "And does she know of Olivia?"

"Yes! Olivia is well, but the other women have shunned her, with the exception of one. An Englishwoman she traveled with had a sister who was killed by the sultan."

Tristan's gut tightened at the memory of the poor woman who had been dragged into the courtyard and violently murdered. "I told you of her death."

The other men nodded slowly. Their expressions reflected the same sadness and disgust at Moulay's actions.

"Apparently, the sister blames Olivia. And, in fact, attacked her."

Tristan's eyes widened. "Was she harmed?"

"Naught more than a bump on the head."

"But why would this woman blame Olivia?" he demanded.

"I have no idea. Neither does Maha, except she says the woman has lost her wits. And she has requested an audience with the sultan, saying she has information regarding Olivia."

Realization struck. "So that is why the sultan questioned the paternity of Olivia's child."

A soldier barged into the room. "The sultan demands his treasure."

"Yes, yes. As I told the sultan, the men on board will never be able to locate it. I must see to it myself."

"I will wait for you in the corridor," the guard stated flatly. He dipped his head, spun around, and left the room. Tristan's mind was filled with a myriad of thoughts. It made sense that he should be able to surrender the gold and jewels and still be able to negotiate the "treaty". That would be the case if the sultan was a reasonable man. Moulay was power-hungry and greedy, but how valuable did he believe an alliance with the English would be? Tristan could only hope the sultan would value it a great deal. In the meantime, Tristan must find a way for them out of this hell.

He turned to Leo. "Can you call for this Maha again? Perhaps she knows of a way out."

Leo's face lit up. "Oh, I think I can manage that."

Tristan rolled his eyes. "Your duty is to help us get out of this place."

"I agree, my lord. But I see no reason to suffer while I glean information." He shrugged. "But, I wonder if we might add another passenger when we leave." Leo worked his jaw as he waited for Tristan's response.

Tristan shrugged. "What is one more? We are all going to die here anyway." And he laughed hollowly. Shaking his head, he moved toward the door to join the waiting soldier.

\*\*\*

Olivia found herself wandering about the room with the fountains. She was, by now, familiar with it, but she had naught else to do to pass the time. She had eaten her fill and the other women were polite but showed no real interest in speaking with her. Loneliness was an oppressor she had to battle. She could not give in to sadness, for it would destroy her determination.

Sabra was suddenly in front of her. "Follow me to the gardens," she said with no preamble.

Olivia was very apprehensive, since she inherently did not trust this woman, but after taking a moment to weigh her options, she decided to do as Sabra requested. They walked down a winding corridor which opened into a magnificent courtyard. An explosion of a myriad of flowers assailed her and Olivia blinked at the nearly overwhelming flare of color. It was so lush and so full of exotic blooms, it didn't appear real. If not for the cloying scent, Olivia might have only conjured this vision. She gasped and Sabra laughed. "It is a lot, at first. But you get used to it. Great care is taken with this area and many of the women take pleasure in tending it." It sounded to Olivia almost like a defense.

"Oh, no, it is glorious. And I appreciate the hours it must take to maintain. I suppose I simply did not expect something so…impressive." Her praise was sincere. She should have discovered this garden sooner, but she was

Leslie Hachtel

not inclined to explore too far with so many watching. "But I wonder if I will ever acclimate to the heat here."

"Your skin is darker than most English, but you seem as frail as the others. You will become accustomed to it and then you will learn to hate the cold and rain you left behind." She motioned with her hand over her shoulder. "Come with me." Sabra led her to a secluded bench in a corner. Tension tightened Olivia's shoulders and she glanced about, vigilant in her worry she could be attacked.

Sabra indicated the seat and smiled. "You may trust me. I just wish to impart information."

Trust. Not so easily given, although Olivia trusted Maha. But Sabra still made the hair on her nape tighten.

Olivia looked at her with expectation and Sabra narrowed her eyes. "Is it true your child is conceived by a married noble."

Olivia scrambled to recall what Tristan had said in her presence. She could not remember this detail and wondered if this was some sort of trap. She dropped her chin and lowered her voice. "You have questioned me on this before. I fear I am not at liberty to disclose the identity of the father."

"I see." Tension tightened Sabra's lips. "But we are friends, are we not? You can confide in me."

Olivia inhaled through her nose. "I am sorry, but I cannot. It is a political issue and there would be consequences."

"So, there is no father, and no child, is there?" Accusation was clear.

"Sabra, there is, of course, a child. I am certain you understand how precarious my position is. The fact that an ambassador was sent here to retrieve me attests to my value, and that of the unborn babe. It is very awkward, however."

112

Sabra's cheeks colored with frustration. "I do not understand. But I was hoping you would tell me what is really happening so I could help."

"Help? How?" Olivia was honestly confused.

"You think because I am not one of the Kadins that I have no power or influence?" Her voice trembled with her resentment.

"Oh, no, I thought no such thing," Olivia soothed. "I value your friendship and would appreciate any advice you offer."

Sabra exhaled, mollified. "Good then, since I intend to rise in the sultan's estimation very soon. Therefore, I will be able to wield power and influence. Even now, I am above so many of the others. And I am very beautiful, do you not agree?"

"Very beautiful," Olivia affirmed. Although she believed beauty should be more than superficial.

"And you agree I should be one of the favorites?"

"Of course. No one, I am sure, is more deserving." She kept her expression neutral.

Olivia could not figure out what was going on here. Was Sabra merely trying to impress her? But why? Did the other woman think Olivia could afford her some benefit? Or, was Sabra trying to trip her up so she could report to the sultan and gain favor? Olivia knew to step very carefully. Unless, the other woman merely wanted to assure herself Olivia was not among her competition, which seemed most likely.

"Again," Olivia restated, "I truly value your friendship and any aid you might offer."

"I am very close with Jaffar." She grinned, but the mirth did not extend to her eyes.

"The head eunuch?"

113

Sabra was pleased that Olivia recognized the reference. "Yes. And, as you must already know, he is a very powerful man."

"I assumed as much, since he is the leader."

"Exactly." Sabra leaned in conspiratorially. "Did you know your companion from England has had Jaffar go to the sultan and tell him you were not to be trusted?"

Nausea roiled in Olivia's gut. She had done nothing but try to help Amelia and her sister and, yet, Amelia continued to hold her responsible for Charlotte's death. This could prove dangerous for her, but also to Amelia. And there was nothing she could do.

"What did she say, precisely?"

Sabra's back straightened. "Well, she instructed Jaffar to tell the sultan that she didn't believe you were with child at all, but that if that were true, the nobleman mentioned could not have fathered the babe."

"Really? And why could he not?"

"She said the man had an accident some time ago and could not sire more children."

Olivia forced herself not to react. "Well, that is simply not true. I can attest to that." And she rubbed her belly for effect.

Sabra watched her intently for a moment, looked pointedly at Olivia's middle-section and shrugged. "There truly is no evidence of the child."

Now it was Olivia's turn to shrug. "I have heard that some women do not show until closer to the time of delivery. Why, my sister-in-law never had visible changes until the last month."

"I suppose that is possible." Sabra scooted closer. "But you could tell me what is truly happening. I will tell no one."

Olivia pretended to be surprised by this. "Truly happening? I understand not."

"Jaffar says the sultan fears this is an English plot. That England seeks to invade us and try and steal the sultan's kingdom. And that you are a spy."

This time she did not have to feign surprise. "That is ridiculous, Sabra. If, indeed, my country planned an invasion, they would not need spies. The English army is virtually invincible. So, you may tell Jaffar to relay to the sultan that his fears are groundless."

"But, of course, you would say that." Sabra lifted an arched eyebrow.

Olivia was losing patience with the other woman, but she was also aware that Sabra could create a myriad of problems if Olivia did not choose her words carefully. Perhaps she could use sympathy. "Sabra, I committed an indiscretion and now carry the result." She peered down at her stomach. "And, although I will love my child, I fear he or she will be labeled a bastard unless the duke can claim the babe. Which is possible. The nobleman wants a son, which he does not have." Olivia did not know enough of the man to know if he even had children, but she was counting on Sabra's lack of knowledge here. "He cared enough to send an ambassador, so he must value this child. And me." She impressed herself by managing the tear coursing down her cheek.

Sabra tilted her head and patted her shoulder. "I believe you. I will tell Jaffar Amelia's imaginings are wrong."

It was suddenly clear that Sabra was trying to glean information to take to the sultan. That explained Sabra's offer of friendship. If she could get Olivia to give her any information the sultan might find useful, she would rise

115

more quickly in the ranks. It would be a coup if she could forewarn the ruler of some British plot. Or some other juicy gossip that Moulay would find worthy. It was all about getting a leg up in the hierarchy here, and Olivia had no doubt as to Sabra's ambition.

From Sabra's reaction, Olivia prayed she had convinced the other woman that she was simply a woman impregnated who was kidnapped in error and wished to go home.

# Chapter Seven

Tristan had been escorted to his ship by two guards. They respectfully waited on deck as Tristan made his way down to his cabin.

"Damn, damn, damn." This was not going as he had hoped. By now, he should have been able to return the treasure, turn over the documents, and be on their way back home. But Tristan had suspected, almost from the beginning, that this game could not be so simply won. Moulay wanted the return of his gold and jewels, and he obviously wanted a treaty with England, but he trusted no one and the negotiations would not be so simple. Tristan wished he had been more skilled, but guile did not come easily to him. He had sensed he needed to withhold as much as possible for as long as possible until he had achieved his goal, but he had no idea as to the sultan's endgame. And he feared for Olivia. He would just have to be smarter than the sultan.

He closed his cabin door and locked it. He lifted the floor panel, revealing the cache. It was indeed a king's ransom, but Moulay thought it his due and would therefore not be particularly grateful to Tristan for its return. Tristan shook his head in frustration and lifted the bags from the hold.

He scooped a handful of gold coins out of one of the

117

bags and, tearing off some of the sheet covering his cot, made a small sack. He slipped that into his shirt, letting it settle against his waist. If they needed to bribe someone, this would be most helpful. Then, he removed a few glittering bracelets and several strands of pearls. He retrieved a large ruby brooch and added that to the pile, along with two rings, one set with sapphires and the other with emeralds. These alone were a king's ransom. He hefted the three purses and they still seemed quite full.

Carefully, he replaced the jewels he had separated beneath the panel and slipped the concealing wood back into place. Tazim would at least have something to show for his suffering. That is, if they ever had the chance to return home.

He gathered the velvet bags and ambled back up on deck. The captain watched expectantly, but

Tristan gave a slight shake of his head to indicate he and the crew should do nothing. Killing

these soldiers would only make the situation worse.

Once Tristan had returned to the sultan's palace, there was no delay this time in being shown into the ruler's presence. Tristan bowed and approached Moulay, laying the bags at his feet. A backward wave of the sultan's hand and two of his men stepped up and lifted the bounty to within Moulay's reach. He opened the first sack, peered inside and a nod indicted his pleasure. He repeated the action with the other two purses, then clapped his hands.

A strange little man immediately appeared. Although his garb was traditional, the vest he wore indicated he had a higher rank than most. It sparkled with gold thread and jewels. Moulay pointed to the bags. "Put these away and see they do not disappear. Again." The threat was clear. "And I wish an inventory. I am hoping nothing is missing."

The small man gave a few quick little jerks of his head and snatched up the bags. Two soldiers trailed him as he scurried from the room.

The sultan then turned his gaze on Tristan. "You have done well to return my property. I suppose I might offer a reward. But then again, some of my property might be lost."

"I have given you all there was from the man who stole it, as promised." Tristan swallowed. He was counting on the fact that the sultan would have no idea exactly what had been taken so many years ago or what had been spent, since as a matter of course some would have been disposed of. "We can go then?" Tristan tried to keep the raw hope contained.

Moulay frowned. "Have you forgotten we must still agree on the treaty?" The accusation hung in the air.

"Of course, of course," Tristan assured him. "I meant after I deliver the parchments and you have accepted."

"And is there any reason I should not accept?"

"No. But a man of your discerning abilities will want to examine the documents, assuring yourself of their value."

"And their authenticity?"

Tristan controlled his reaction to this. The old man was clever. "There will be no doubt as to their legitimacy."

"Unlike the child the woman carries." The sultan narrowed his eyes, then tilted his head. Was this an attempt at humor? Or did he already know something? Had a physician been summoned and reported to the sultan? Tristan tamped down the nausea that threatened.

"The reward I have in mind is a meeting with the woman," the sultan continued. "I have no doubt you would like to reassure her negotiations are in progress."

Truly? Moulay was going to allow him some time with Olivia? The very thought made his pulse quicken, but also set his teeth on edge. The sultan did not reward people out of compassion unless he received something in return. "Thank you, Great One. Your kindness is much appreciated."

\*\*\*

Olivia wondered how the other women here tolerated their lives. Their minds had to have grown fallow, since no one ever read a book. Some recited poetry, but it seemed they had no understanding of the words they spoke. Many spent their time bathing and eating and resting on chaises. Some strummed instruments. Occasionally, several of them would dance. They oiled themselves and applied kohl to their eyes. They were massaged and strolled in the garden. But they were confined. Beautiful birds in a golden cage. And, of course, most were without plumage. Olivia wondered if she could ever get used to the others and their lack of clothing.

The lack of activity was driving Olivia to distraction. She ached to gallop her horse across the meadow. Or go for a walk alone along the hillside. Or even embroider a new collar. She also desperately missed sitting at a table and sharing a meal with her family, curling up in the library with an interesting novel. Having a meaningful conversation where she needn't weigh every word spoken. She yearned to be free.

Powerlessness weighed on her, enveloping her like heavy chains, and everything in her longed to rebel. But she could find no opportunity. And she was well aware disobedience or the obvious troublemakers were dealt with severely. She worried about Tristan, her family, her new friend Braheem. She had not seen Braheem in days and she wondered why he was absent. Asking for him might put him under suspicion and she did not wish to put him at risk.

***

It had become Olivia's habit to break her fast early in the morning before many of the others had risen from sleep. She would fill a plate and, after exchanging pleasantries with some of the others, wander out into the garden to eat. It had become her sanctuary. The strange and unusual birds sang among the branches of fruit trees and the vivid colors and fragrances were soothing, if still a bit overpowering. And the early morning sun was not so brutal as it was later in the day.

This morning, Maha sought her out. She sidled up to Olivia and took a seat next to her.

"Good morning," Olivia greeted her, but she could see the other woman was vibrating with eagerness.

"Yes, it is." Maha leaned in closer and whispered conspiratorially. "He loves me. He said so." She heaved a sigh and sat back. "He promised we shall all be free and soon."

"You must be speaking of Leo."

"There is no other. And he cares not I have been here for years and was not untouched."

Olivia smiled broadly. "I am glad. Did he say there was a plan?"

"He said they would decide how to do it and I should not worry."

The words of a man who was in love. No substance

121

and naught to rely on. Merely dreams of a future that may or may not come to pass.

After a moment of silence, Maha straightened her spine and there was a glint in her eyes. She seemed happy or at least relieved by something. "There is news."

Olivia raised an eyebrow expectantly. "News?"

"One of the Kadins has fallen ill."

Now, Olivia was confused. "This pleases you?" She had hoped her new friend would show compassion if another of their number was sick.

"Oh, Veva is the meanest one. Her name means 'leader of the tribe' and she always took it to heart. Of late, she is losing her beauty and works daily to enhance it, but she is fading. And she takes it out on all the servants. We are not sorry she has weakened and will not beat us—at least until she recovers."

It made sense. No one wanted to see the cruel have the strength to punish, especially if it was undeserved.

"What does this mean for the harem?"

"There must always be four favorites. With Veva unavailable, another will take her place. The sultan will begin to call for women and when he finds one that pleases him, he will choose another favorite. It is simple. So now, all the women will vie for that position. There will be much grooming and preening and I will be kept very busy." She lowered her voice and inched closer. "I have heard that Sabra's ambition might be responsible."

"Would Sabra actually sicken someone to advance herself here?" Olivia found the idea frightening.

"Sabra would sell her own mother for a chance at being one of the favorites." Trying to glean information was one thing, but making another ill? Olivia exhaled her disgust. This was truly hell on earth.

\*\*\*

Early the next morning, one of the eunuchs appeared in Olivia's room. With a tilt of his head, he indicated she was to follow him. He pointed to her veil, and lifted his finger. She was to leave the harem? Anticipation mixed with trepidation and the hair on her arms rose. Her heart thumped against her ribs. She quickly dressed and covered her face with the fabric. Tamping down the terror of uncertainty, she went with the man. Had the sultan called for her? Was she to be among those considered as a favorite? No, she was supposed to be with child, so she would have no appeal for him.

He led her outside into the courtyard and across to the main part of the palace. The opulence was breathtaking. A rainbow of colors and patterns and silken drapes might have created the image of dreams, if this had not been a nightmare.

They marched down one corridor after another until, finally, the man stopped and held out his arm. She peered into the space. It was not a large room, but it was darker than most, and cool. Light peeked across the ceiling from high windows, casting dancing shadows over the tiled walls. Cushions were everywhere. In the center was a table set with fruits and nuts and the odd bread they consumed here. A dish of olives gleamed next to a bowl of oil. Olivia's mouth watered, but she was so unsure of the circumstances, she dared not move. She eased into the room and stood, waiting.

Her eyes searched for a means of escape, but that would be futile. Where would she go? She had no idea in what direction lay the sea and only the heartless desert surrounded them on the other sides. Her breath came in small gasps as she tried to control her rising panic.

A pair of hands were laid on her shoulders and she stiffened, terrified to turn and see who touched her. But she was spun around and her veil was lifted as lips pressed against her own. Lips she had felt before. Could it be? She opened her eyes as she pulled slightly back. Deep blue eyes were smiling into her own and she nearly collapsed with relief which quickly changed to utter joy. Tristan!

She threw her arms around his neck and pressed herself against him. It was like coming home. Her body melted against his, inhaling his masculine scent. She tucked her head against his muscled chest and then raised her face to his for another kiss. This one was full of longing and spoke of her need for him. He answered with a passion that weakened her knees and set her blood throbbing.

Tristan ended the kiss and pulled her toward some pillows that lay against the far wall. He sank down and drew her with him. She curled against him like a cat, wanting to get ever closer. Stroking her back, Tristan lowered his mouth to her ear.

"Are you well?" Concern in his voice warmed her.

"I am. Are you?"

"Merely irritated. Until now. Seeing you makes everything so much better." He kissed her again and she melted into him. The kiss broken, he blew out a breath. "I had hoped we would be done here by now and I would be escorting you home. But the sultan appears to take pleasure in the frustration of others."

"He takes pleasure in doing more than that," she whispered. A shiver shook her to her bones.

Tristan leaned back, his body stiff. "Has he harmed you?"

"No. Not me. One of the women I came with."

He nodded solemnly. "The woman with light hair?"

"You saw her?"

"Yes," he responded in a whisper. "I watched her die." He inhaled a breath. "It was terrible."

"We must be careful. I am certain we are watched," Olivia said, pulling slightly away, but unwilling to break total contact.

She was almost afraid to ask the next question. "Tristan, my family? Are they well? Were they harmed when I was taken? I need to make certain."

"Yes, I know it was cryptic before, but they are all well. Nabil is dead." With those words, a weight was lifted from her.

"How?" she asked, anxious for the details to assure herself it was true.

"He took Catherine from her room and threatened young Malcolm, but Catherine took the villain down with a hairpin, of all things…" He smiled at the thought of her sister's ingenuity and bravery. She closed her eyes, pride in her sister filling her.

"Your brother and Tazim finished the others. What they had no way of knowing was that you were at risk as well. You know they would have protected you at all costs."

"I know that. I do not blame them. I am just so thankful they are all unscathed." He could not have brought her more wonderful news. Unless it was that they were free to go.

"You have an amazing family. And soon, you will all be reunited."

"I have faith in you." She looked into his sea-blue eyes and a wash of adoration lifted her heart. "You have come for me. There are no words to tell you of my love."

"I could do nothing else." He gently stroked her cheek with the back of his hand.

"What does the sultan demand for our release?" There was desperation in her question.

"Well, I have already given him the treasure."

"Treasure? Tazim's treasure?"

Tristan smiled. "Well, officially, I suppose it *did* belong to the sultan."

Her brother-in-law had suffered so much and was finally able to claim some gain for his misery. And he had sent it with Tristan, for her. Gratitude at his generosity suffused her. But she also felt guilty. Tazim had given so much for her.

"He said you were worth far more and we knew it could be used as a bargaining tool."

Such selflessness brought tears to her eyes. "Again, there are no words." She brought her gaze to his. "But if you surrendered the treasure, why are we not free?" It made no sense.

"We believed the sultan would view return of his gold and jewels as his due. It was done to soften his attitude. But no one really thought it would be enough."

"So, what now?" She bit her lower lip.

"I also brought a parchment promising a treaty with England." He stroked her hair and comforted her with his touch.

Olivia's eyebrows shot up. "The king agreed to this?"

Tristan smiled and put his mouth next to her ear. She tingled with his breath. They dare not be overheard. "Not exactly. But your sister has a gift for fancy writing, and we have used that to our advantage."

Olivia pulled back, aghast. "What if Moulay discovers it is a forgery?" she whispered.

Tristan shook his head. "I am more concerned he will realize you are not with child."

Olivia dropped her chin. "I know. I have stuffed scarves around my waist, but I am quite sure many suspect the truth."

"So we must complete this business before the sultan finds out the truth. He has already threatened an examination and I am not clear if he means to have a physician come examine you."

"Then we must surely get away before that comes to pass." Bile climbed into her throat at the thought of their deception being uncovered.

"I know." Tristan reached over and caressed her cheek. "I have missed you so much."

She leaned into the touch. "I love you, Tristan. You have put your own life at risk for me."

"I have no life without you." He angled down and his mouth touched her, gently at first, then with a demand for more. His tongue slipped between her lips and mated with hers and the kiss deepened. She was becoming lost in his embrace. He drew her tighter against him and she could feel his manhood against her thigh. Her own core quickened and pulsated.

With no corset or traditional undergarments to restrict him, he slid his hand up to her breast and cupped it under the thin fabric. She closed her eyes and inhaled sharply as he massaged her flesh and never wanted him to stop. In fact, she wanted more. Wantonly, she arched her back to allow him better access. He held her, then gently eased her away.

When she opened her eyes, mindful her heart was beating nearly out of her chest, Tristan was smiling at her. He kissed her again very gently and sat back, leaning on his forearms.

She was confused and in awe of her reaction to him. She scooted nearer to him and rested her body against his. His arms came around her and pulled her closer. His nearness was so wonderful. Olivia wished she could stay like this forever, in the sanctuary of his arms. Only in some other place, of course.

"We dare not do more. I only wished to show you my love and desire. It may take longer than anticipated to get you away from here, and I wanted you to have something to remember me by."

She immediately sobered. "Tristan, we cannot delay. You know this, as well as I. The good news is Bekir's twin brother is here."

He cocked his head. "Bekir?"

"The man who helped Catherine when she was fleeing from here. He married Shera's maid, Poppy."

"I remember now. He has a twin?"

She nodded and smiled. "His name is Braheem and he will help us. He is one of the eunuchs in the harem."

"It is good to have allies. It should make the road easier." She squeezed his hand but worried he wasn't convinced the road would ever get easier.

"Well...there also might be a slight complication. I agreed to help one of the women." She dropped her gaze.

"Help? What does that mean exactly?" He lifted her chin with his finger.

"I promised to take her with us."

"Which woman?"

"Her name is Maha. She has hair like Shera's."

"You, too?" Hi mouth dropped open. "She extracted that promise from Leo, as well. She is no doubt desperate to be gone from this place. But, of course, who can blame her?"

"She has had a terrible life and she, well, I think she has truly become enamored of Leo."

Tristan blew out a breath. "Leo feels the same about her. So, I suppose we will have no choice."

Footsteps outside the room had them both straightening. Quickly, Tristan reached inside his shirt and pulled out the pouch full of gold which he then pressed into her hand.

"Tuck this away."

She slipped it inside her waistband as a soldier appeared at the entrance, glaring at them.

"Do you think he saw us?" Olivia asked, her voice quivering. "He frowns so."

"He always looks like that. They all do. But then, how could anyone be happy with the threat of the sultan's sword hanging over them."

"What can I do to help you?" she whispered, hoping against hope there was already a successful strategy in place that he hadn't felt confident enough to share.

"I am certain the sultan dares not risk the enmity of our country. That is in our favor. But he seems to want to delay our release. Once I know his motive, I can see to your freedom. Trust me, it is all I think about." He lifted his hand to touch her again, then refrained. It would not help if he was seen caressing her. "Go now and be patient. It will be soon."

Reluctantly, she stood and smoothed her garments. With one last look over her shoulder, she plodded over to the guard who led her back to the harem.

\*\*\*

Restlessness would not allow her to sit and wait, so she strolled out into the garden. The afternoon sun washed over her like a bath of hot honey and she lifted her face to it. So unlike home where the days like this were few and far between. Olivia wandered along the paths, idly sniffing various blooms, her thoughts scattered. She had faith in Tristan, but they had both been thrust into such a hostile environment. Could they ever truly find their way out?

Voices ahead of her slowed her pace—a man and a woman. Olivia drew closer. From her vantage point, Olivia could see them, but she was concealed from their view. She recognized the woman. Amelia. A man sat beside her, holding her hand and she leaned her head toward his chest. But something was wrong. Hand holding? Affection? It made no sense. Abruptly, he stood, and Olivia was surprised by his height.

From his garments, she deduced he was a eunuch, but he was huge. He turned and she recognized Jaffar. The same man who had watched over Amelia and brought her food the other day. Did she really require such intent guarding? Or was Jaffar, for some reason, very over-protective?

He towered over Amelia and, for a moment just stared at her with an inscrutable expression. Was his intent to harm her now? Could Olivia stop him? But before she could move, he slid his hand under the other woman's elbow and lifted her as if she were made of the most fragile of materials. A smile creased his dark face and very white teeth caught the light of the sun. He was acting the lovesick swain.

Amelia angled her head down and to the side, so her visage was not visible to Jaffar. But Olivia could see her clearly. She was sneering. Then, her features softened, and she pasted a smile on her face as she turned back to him. She reached up to slip her hand into the crook of his arm. After seeing the other woman's expression, Olivia knew the madness was feigned. The woman was as sane as she was.

Jaffar was clearly very protective of his charge and carefully led her down an adjacent path. She followed meekly, and when she stumbled, he immediately steadied her. The action of a man in love. Or, at least, one completely besotted. When his face came into better view, Olivia recognized it was more than mere infatuation. Jaffar's expression was one of raw hunger. So, to take a man's parts clearly did not take away his heart. It was very sad he had no idea how Amelia felt about him. It would destroy him. Amelia was more than dangerous.

Olivia found she was no longer worried about Amelia. She shivered, realizing Jaffar could be a real threat if he believed Amelia's lies about her. He was the head eunuch, which gave him privilege and no doubt favor from Moulay, as well as access. Digesting this new information, she made her way back to the main area and sat at what had become her favorite place next to one of the fountains. Her thoughts circled, reaching for some solution, some means of escape from all this. But it only seemed things were worsening.

She had not been sitting long when Braheem passed by her and she could tell he wished her to follow. Waiting until she was sure no one was paying attention, she slowly made her way to the corridor on the side of the room.

"You were seen," he hissed.

"What?" Olivia was baffled. "Seen where?"

"With the ambassador. You were watched. The sultan knows the man caressed you." Braheem shook his head at this, indicating it could be calamity.

Olivia panicked. "Did the spy see anything else?"

"No. He was only able to see the ambassador hold you. If you had been seen kissing, you would be dead by now."

Olivia raised her hands to her cheeks. "No! How could we be so stupid?" Anger at herself vibrated through her.

131

"It is my fault. I should have been here to warn you. But Jaffar has seen to it I had one task after another."

"Jaffar is in love with Amelia," she whispered.

Braheem's mouth opened into a wide 'O'. "What? How do you know?"

"I saw him with her in the garden. There is no doubt he is enamored."

Braheem heaved a sigh. "Then that presents yet another problem. If he truly believes her lies, or shows her respect by abiding by her words, he is lost to us. I was hoping to enlist his aid."

"Would he have helped otherwise?" Olivia tilted her head in question.

"Jaffar's loyalty is usually sold to the highest bidder. Moulay knows this and keeps him fat. But, no man like him is ever satisfied, so he is always open to a bribe. But, perhaps not in this case."

"There is more. Amelia is but playing at madness. I saw how she looked at Jaffar when he was not watching. She is quite sane. I now believe she is using him to her own ends. Although I have no idea what her plan is."

"I fear she wishes to somehow manage to place herself in a better position. And, if it is as you say—and I have no reason to doubt you—Jaffar will do anything to help her. Even going to the sultan as many times as she deems necessary to accomplish her ends."

Olivia shook her head. "I am usually a good judge of character. If I had not seen it for myself, I would have continued to worry about Amelia and feel pity for her."

"You are soft-hearted. I am certain you always see the best in others." He patted his own chest for emphasis.

"What will happen now?" Worry creased her brow. "If the sultan believes the ambassador and I are in love, he will question everything. Tristan, I mean the ambassador, will lose all credibility. And the sultan will retaliate. I have no doubt he is not a man who will tolerate being made a fool." Olivia pressed her hands to her temples.

"The sultan is as clever as a jackal. He is never to be underestimated. Even the years have not dimmed his abilities. So, he will use any information he is given to his advantage."

Olivia sucked on her lower lip. "Which means he will doubt I am in love with another nobleman."

"In which case, you are either lying about carrying a child or you are a…" He obviously could not voice the name.

"Whore," she provided, nodding.

"Yes. And either way, you will have no more value." He grabbed her upper arms, his brows drawn together. "We must get you out of here as quickly as possible."

"But how?"

"I have promised to protect you, and I will keep that vow at all costs. Do not worry, my lady. I will come up with something."

"What of the secret passages? Is there any way we can use them to our benefit?" She so wished this to be a solution.

"I have already thought of that. I can get you out of the harem, but since one of the sultan's concubines escaped that way, the path is guarded. I am still trying to find a way to get you to the ship without interference. I have not given up that idea. But there are other ways. And I will find them." He nodded his affirmation.

She smiled at him. "Between you and the ambassador, I believe you will succeed." She prayed this was true. Time was running out.

133

# Chapter Eight

Tristan and his two companions were escorted into the presence of Moulay early the next morning. He was again standing in the middle of the courtyard surrounded by a group of pale, quaking men. Sweat dripped off those waiting and pooled onto the stones at their feet and Tristan doubted it had anything to do with the heat of the day. It was no wonder, since the sultan was dressed in red. Leo and Felix knew the significance of the red cloak. Both men were coiled tight, containing their defenses, but ready to protect Tristan. They were aware that any wrong move could mean they would all die.

The sun, that glorious orb, completely oblivious of the world beneath it, lit the sky with golden rays. If it had been aware, it would no doubt have hidden behind a cloud in shame.

The sultan paced back and forth, back and forth, swinging a scimitar boasting a wicked blade. It caught the sun's beams and flashed light into one man's eyes. Perhaps it was a blessing that the man squinted against the bright rays as the sword sang its melody of death. He fell to his knees, then slumped flat onto the ground. Two soldiers sprang forward and dragged the lifeless corpse away. Tristan was certain the two who took the body away would never return to the courtyard if they had a choice. A glance at several other soldiers' faces told Tristan they believed themselves to be safe and they were actually thriving off the residual power. It tightened his gut.

No one else in the line of men moved, but urine stained several of the men's pants as tears coursed down their cheeks. The tremoring of men in mortal terror shook the tiles beneath their feet. Death hovered expectantly, greedily, as if the edge of the weapon was the serpent's tongue and might strike at any moment. The waiting, the uncertainty, was nearly as terrible as the outcome.

Tristan stood with Felix and Leo, sickened by this scene, but all three determined by unspoken agreement they could not show weakness. That would only serve to demean rather than save them. Tristan said a prayer for Olivia. *If I die, please God, save her. See her home to her family.*

The sultan slithered over to the three who waited on the side and stopped, a demonic grin splitting his face. He lifted his sword above his head and gazed triumphantly at Tristan and his companions. None of the three moved, or even flinched. The sultan's lips tightened, and his eyes narrowed. He took a step back and swung the vicious weapon and the servant next to Leo crumpled to the earth. Tristan felt, rather than saw the brothers tighten every muscle in their bodies to force themselves to stand firm. He, too, dug his nails into his palms and refused to bow to the utter unspeakable fear that had turned his insides to jelly.

The sultan hesitated a mere moment, nodded as if he approved and strode off into the palace.

No one breathed. Then, slowly, as if they were terrified Moulay would return and take more victims from those running away, the men inched their way from the courtyard to resume their duties. Soon, all but four guards remained and these surrounded Tristan and his companions. Understanding they were to be escorted inside, Tristan nodded at Leo and Felix and they allowed themselves to be led into the palace. Once inside, the brothers were ushered away, while Tristan was directed into the presence of Moulay.

The sultan appeared completely unperturbed by the recent events. He had changed into a cloak of yellow, but otherwise appeared as if naught had transpired but a few moments ago. Obviously, the lives of the people who served him had no more meaning for him than a minor amusement that passed the time. Shock at this penetrated and Tristan was sickeningly aware he was dealing with a madman. But a very clever madman with too much power at his command.

Why did the soldiers not rebel? It had to be torment to stand waiting for the sword to fall. And yet, Tristan understood the men feared Moulay as one might show reverence for God himself. And who would dare challenge God?

"You have lied to me." The sultan spoke the words without intonation.

"Great One? I have not lied. I do not understand." He frowned in consternation. But he knew he and Olivia had been seen and it was reported to Moulay.

"Is it your child she carries? Or does she carry one at all?" Moulay's accusation was sharp.

"I—"

But Moulay cut him off. "Do not bother to come up with more falsehoods. I have indeed decided upon an examination. My physician is on his way even as we speak." The sultan looked down his nose. "And all of your deceptions will be uncovered." He grinned and licked his lips. "If she is with child, I will see to it she tells me who the father is." He grinned again and Tristan's skin tightened. The sultan did not need to elaborate on how he could make people talk. Tristan was certain he could imagine.

It was over. A weight as heavy as a thousand stones pressed down on him. They would all die here. He had only one hope: to continue to lie more and bluff his way into convincing Moulay. It was a tiny thread to hang onto, but it was all Tristan had.

"There was no deception, Great One. If what you were told was that I offered comfort to her, it was only because she needed reassurance. She is understandably frightened and wishes to go home."

"So you did not caress her?"

Tristan remembered how he felt when John had accused him of dishonoring Olivia. He managed to reflect that outrage. "Caress her? And risk all?" That was too true. "If the Duke thought I had laid a hand on her, my life would be forfeit. No, Great One. She was crying, as women are prone to do, especially in this condition. I merely offered a shoulder to receive her tears."

The sultan ruminated on this. There was still the treaty hanging in the balance and it was foolish for him to ignore the possibilities it might offer. And he was not a man given to foolishness.

"We shall see what the physician reports." The sultan waved his hand and Tristan was dismissed.

Tristan's heart sank to his knees. A doctor would certainly know that she carried naught in her womb. He offered a prayer that God would help them.

*** 

Olivia dozed in her room. The constant fear and tension had exhausted her, and the only respite was in sleep. Suddenly, she was shaken awake. Her eyes flew open and Braheem was kneeling next to her cot. Her hands crossed over her chest, trying to still her pounding heart.

"Do you have any money?" he demanded.

The words shocked her. "What?" He wanted money from her?

As if he read her thoughts, he shook his head. "For the physician. He has been sent for."

She jumped up so quickly, dizziness clouded her thoughts. The import of this took a moment to penetrate. Her breath caught and her mouth went dry. "A physician?" It took her less than a breath of time for the full weight of that to sink in. Her blood ran cold. "To verify I carry a child." It was not a question.

"Yes. But, there is good news. The man does not have any affection for the sultan. He and his family have not been well-treated. But he is also a man who values what he can gain from a situation."

Olivia nodded her understanding. "Which is why you asked if I have money?"

"Precisely." Braheem allowed a small smile to lift his lips.

"Do you really think he will verify my condition?" She frowned, unsure if they could trust this.

Braheem's grin grew wider. "I was actually thinking of another condition."

"Another condition? I understand not." Now she was getting worried.

Braheem angled to her and explained, keeping his

voice very low. "You have no doubt heard Veva has taken ill."

"Yes, I know."

"Did you also know there is naught the sultan fears more than contagious illness?"

"Does Veva suffer from some plague?"

"My guess is a potion delivered to her by one of her servants. One with ambition."

Olivia wasn't surprised. She'd known this type of behavior was common here, but it brought home to her just how vicious the women could be. Survival here was precarious at best.

"That is terrible." Olivia heaved out a breath.

"You are quite naïve," he responded, his hands tented under his chin. "Since the beginning of time, the easiest way to rid yourself of a rival was to kill them." His tone was now very matter-of-fact. "But when one falls mysteriously ill here, it is immediately reported to Moulay. He then must be reassured it is nothing he can catch. If it is reported to be poison, he cares not. But if it something else…"

"This is an abysmal place." Desolation swept through her like a dark wind. Nausea threatened and all she wanted was for Tristan to take her home. She closed her eyes and prayed for strength. "Feeling sorry for myself will not help, I know, but Braheem…" She huffed out her frustration.

"We were speaking of illness," he reminded her. "And the sultan's fear of it."

She furrowed her brow. "Yes. But what has that to do with me?"

"The physician will not come for several days, since there is no rush and the sultan enjoys delaying tactics."

"Go on." She was almost afraid of what he was going to suggest.

"Well, Veva's illness gave me an inspiration."

"An inspiration that requires a bribe?" she asked.

"Exactly. If you were to come down with some terrible disease that you brought from England, something that the sultan could catch, he would wish all of you gone." He lifted his shoulders and dropped them again. "In fact, he would immediately leave the palace with only his favorites until he could be assured there was no longer a danger. And he would evict anyone from here who might carry the sickness."

A smile teased her mouth. "A very dreadful sickness. One that is highly contagious. Yes. I agree." Her mind was whirling with ideas. This was brilliant. "But will the physician agree and confirm this?"

"That is the best part," Braheem affirmed. "It would give him great pleasure to instill terror into the sultan. For a fee, of course."

"Of course." A thought occurred. "Do you think the servant who tended me might be stricken, too?"

He shook his head. "I imagine the sultan would not care if Maha accompanied you. She has been exposed to the man with the ambassador, as well as you. The sultan would happily be rid of her."

Olivia clapped her hands in delight. "Truly, there are no secrets in the harem." She angled closer and lowered her voice conspiratorially. "So we must be careful." Excitement thrummed through her and she wanted to jump up and dance about. But, of course, she dare not. After all, she was a very sick woman. And she could barely stifle her giggle at the thought. "I must tell Maha."

"Be cautious. I think no one should be told until the

doctor has come and gone. If anyone were to find out, all would be lost."

"I agree, I will tell no one. And I cannot thank you enough." She took his hand. It was so soft for a man, and it reminded her of all he had suffered. "But what of you, Braheem? Do you wish to remain here?"

His expression grew very solemn. "Yes. I have dedicated myself to helping when I can." He lowered his voice. "And subverting the desires of the sultan. He is a vicious and heartless man, but who is to say if his successor would be any better. So, the only hope for the ones destined to remain here is to have someone sympathetic who can offer respite whenever possible. It is my true destiny." His dark eyes lit up. "And now that I know, thanks to you, that Jaffar is in love, his days as head eunuch will be numbered. A eunuch in love with one of his charges changes loyalty. He will make mistakes and can no longer be relied upon."

She raised an eyebrow. "Will you take his place?"

He grinned. "Do you doubt it?"

\*\*\*

"More fragrant oil." The demand echoed through the large area and several of the women clustered together and began whispering among themselves. The order came from Sabra, who was stretched out naked on a long table covered with soft linens. Maha scurried over with a small vial. Another servant took the aromatic vessel and, pouring some into her hand, massaged it into Sabra's bare shoulders.

Maha had tears in her eyes as she swept past Olivia, intent on an errand. Olivia followed her and whispered, "What is happening?"

"She is to be the sultan's new favorite, no matter how many she has to walk on to get there." Maha inhaled to contain a sob. "Or poison."

Olivia was no longer shocked by this. "Isn't the favorite the sultan's choice?"

"Yes and no. He will call for women to be brought and Sabra has paid well for the privilege of being the first. And seeing to reducing the number of her rivals. Did you hear that three more of the gedikli have taken ill?"

A wave of sympathy for them washed over Olivia. "No. Will no one stop her?"

Maha gave her a look of disbelief. "How? All would need to stop eating and drinking."

Of course, Sabra was clever enough to find a way. So, Sabra was not only ambitious. She was also, like the sultan, bloodthirsty. What kind of a world was this? Killing without punishment. Personal desire striking anyone who stands in the way.

"Now Sabra prepares herself so she will not be rejected." Maha shuddered. Olivia knew Maha's thoughts were of the abuse to come.

A loud order interrupted them. "Maha, come massage my feet!" And Maha dragged herself over to the shrew.

Olivia shook her head in sympathy for Maha and the others and wished she could take Maha into her confidence. She would be thrilled to know her days in service here were numbered. But Olivia must heed Braheem's advice. Any slip of the tongue and they would all be in mortal danger.

As she passed one of the groups of women, Olivia heard a few choice words to describe Sabra. None of them were flattering.

# Chapter Nine

This could not go on much longer. The sultan had not sent for Tristan and he had no way of knowing what was going on in the man's mind. Had the physician already examined Olivia? It had already been two miserable days of uncertainty. Did the sultan know her womb was empty? Had he punished her for the lie? Then when would the soldiers come for him and his men? Could they do naught but sit pathetically like lambs going to the slaughter?

His patience worn thin, he had sent one of the soldiers to request an audience, but the man had not returned, and Tristan wanted to crawl out of his skin. If they were all to die, he wanted to know.

He strode over to another one of the guards that stood at attention by the entrance to his rooms.

"May I ask you a question?" he addressed the man in Arabic.

The soldier shrugged indifferently.

"If I needed a doctor, how long would it take for him to come and tend me." He tried to keep any emotion from his voice. Mayhap the physician would take some more time and the secret remained undiscovered.

"The soldier looked at him with a modicum of interest. "And are you ill? For if that is the case, I must inform the sultan as to the nature of your sickness."

143

Unsure of how to answer, Tristan opted for continuing the subterfuge. "My stomach is painful to me."

The guard frowned, clearly deciding what to do with this information. "I can request a doctor to come. Unless it is the sultan himself, the man is never in a great hurry. It might be a day or so or more."

Tristan found that reassuring. "Well, let us wait until tomorrow. If my pain does not improve, I will ask for him to visit me."

The guard straightened his spine and returned to staring ahead into space. Tristan spun on his heel and paced back into the apartment. Leo came striding into the room with Felix directly behind him.

"News?" Tristan demanded.

"Nothing." Leo flung out his arms in irritation.

"I heard some of the men talking. The physician has not yet come," Felix added, "but he is expected tomorrow."

Tristan blew out the breath he didn't realize he'd been holding. "Which gives us one more day to find a way out of this place." He sank down onto his bed and the others sat beside him. A cloud of utter powerlessness, pressed in. Angry at his own lack of ideas in this, Tristan sat up. "We must come up with something. Think!"

The brothers looked at him with a combination of sorrow and defeat. But Tristan was determined there had to be a way.

"We have explored the layout of the palace and it is so well guarded, we could not slip out unnoticed. And even if we could, there is Olivia to consider," Tristan said.

"And Maha," Leo added.

"Yes, yes and Maha," Tristan acknowledged. "I have questioned the soldiers and cannot find one who would dare aid us. But I refuse to accept defeat. We came to rescue Olivia and not die in the process. And we will find a way." If only he could see the sultan, perhaps he could come up with something to convince the man to free them. If there was no escape by stealth, perhaps they could manage with cunning.

***

It was just before dawn and Olivia was already up and dressed, sleep being elusive. The gold and pink hues that heralded the beginning of the day streamed in from a window above the corridor and painted the mosaics outside her small space with dancing light. She hoped the happy colors were an omen for success.

Braheem slipped into her room, his finger to his lips. "The physician comes today. I will greet him and offer him your gift. I will then tell him of your distress."

She grinned, then solemnly nodded. "What exactly is my distress?" she asked.

"Plague, of course. And so the spots will have appeared." He held out a small pot of thick red face paint. Olivia imagined it was usually used in small amounts to heighten the color of the cheeks. She smiled as she reached for the stain.

"Oh, and I can see terrible circles under your eyes and in the hallows of your cheeks." He presented a stick of kohl.

"I must be very ill." She tried not to giggle with delight.

"Oh, I can assure you, you are," he said with mock seriousness. "Prepare yourself and after a while, I will send Maha to tend you. She will, of course, be terrified of the disease you carry, but you must make certain not to

145

reassure her until after the doctor has taken his leave. She must convince him this is very believable. Or, at least real enough to assuage his fear of the sultan."

"Thank you, Braheem."

"This is not over until you are safely aboard the ship with the other English. Then you can be grateful."

"How can I ever thank you?" There would never be a way to properly express her gratitude to this man.

"Live a good life away from this place and tell my brother I am well and happy for him." A faraway look shown in his eyes.

"I will." Her heart ached for this man who truly owed her nothing and was yet risking so much.

Wasting no time, she dotted her face and chest with red marks. Realization of the deception caused her hands to shake. If the sultan discovered this ruse, his fury would know no bounds. But what other choice was there?

She took a deep breath to muster her courage. Then, wiping her fingers, she rubbed the kohl onto the tips and brushed it under her eyes and into the hollows of her cheeks. She had no mirror, so she had to hope the effect was believable. Tucking the makeup under her mattress, she was certain it would not be found. No one would go searching through her room when the threat of disease lingered. And afterward, they would be long gone. Olivia laid back on the cot, dropping her arm over the edge. She intended to look pitiful and prayed she succeeded.

She had completed her disguise none too soon. Two of the eunuchs entered the room as soon as she had pulled up the bedcover and, taking one look at her, gasped and took a step back. Olivia tried not to smile. Instead, she emitted a groan of agony. It sounded real to her ears and the men looked stricken.

"Can you walk?" asked one of the guards, his trepidation clear in the wavering of his voice. Neither man wished to touch her and they made no effort to move closer.

"With help, perhaps," she replied, trying to sound very weak. "Where must I go? I do not believe I can travel far. I do not feel well."

The guards kept backing away as far as they could. Slowly, Olivia pulled herself up, fell back and then lifted again, moving very carefully. As she lurched forward, the two danced even further away. She pretended to stumble in her "weakened" state, and they would have let her fall had she not righted herself.

*I am very good at this. I should have been a mummer.* She was reassuring herself and the effort helped.

She dragged her feet and kept grabbing at the walls for support as she was led down the corridor, out into a small courtyard. The sun was very bright and hot and she prayed it would not melt her makeup. But they were not outside for long. The guards strode ahead of her into a small building off to the side. Her eyes took a moment to adjust to the dim interior. A few steps further and the men stopped at a doorway, motioning her inside. As she passed, they pressed against the

frame lest she come in contact with them.

It was a small room crowded with three beds, a chair and a table. The table was only wide enough to hold a satchel. She immediately surmised this was a makeshift sick room and tried not to feel overly confident. There was still the physician to convince.

Olivia shuffled over to one of the beds and fell upon it, appearing completely exhausted.

Satisfied, the guards retreated to the outside walls,

again as far as possible from Olivia, and stood with rigid backs, waiting.

It was then that Maha stepped into the room and, after taking one look at Olivia, paled and cried out. "My lady? Oh, no, my lady. You are stricken. You have…oh, no." She froze in place, just staring at Olivia. "Forgive me," she whispered. Maha turned on her heel to run out, but the physician filled the entryway. He was an old man with dark skin wrinkled like dried leather. He had a shock of white hair that seemed all the brighter against his brown face. His eyes, though, were those of a man with great intellect. Olivia prayed he had accepted the bribe, for if he had not, there would be no convincing him of anything other than the facts. She would be exposed as a fraud, neither ill nor with child, and she had no doubt the sultan would murder her for her deceptions.

"Stand over there," the physician directed Maha to the far wall. She dropped her head and immediately obeyed. Olivia could not help but notice the tears streaming down her face. She hated that Maha was so frightened, but it could not be avoided.

The doctor approached Olivia, placed his palm on her forehead, and straightened. "You're burning up."

He examined parts of her skin. "Do you itch?" he asked.

"Yes. Terribly," she responded weakly.

"How do you feel?" he asked, his tone very professional.

"Very ill," she whispered. "It hurts, everywhere."

"No doubt. And you are clearly very contagious." He turned to one of the eunuchs. "This woman is stricken with a dangerous illness. She must be kept from anyone who has not already come in direct contact with her.

Those that might have touched her must be separated from the others. At once," he added for emphasis. If she didn't know better, Olivia herself might believe she was contaminated.

"The sultan must be informed immediately," stated one of the guards, his eyes wide, and ran out to do just that. The other soldier hesitated but a trice before running behind his companion.

"Yes," the doctor called loudly to their retreating backs. "Definitely inform the sultan."

He turned back to Olivia. "I fear you will not recover *here,*" he said. "I will meet with Moulay immediately and arrange to have you moved." And leaning in, he winked at her, straightened, and left. Olivia breathed a huge sigh of relief and relaxed, unaware until then how tense her muscles had been.

It was then she became aware of Maha's soft sobbing.

"Maha," she whispered, holding out her hand. Maha approached reluctantly, looking at the proffered appendage as if it were a venomous snake.

"You will not sicken. I promise." Olivia said this very quietly and smiled.

Maha lifted her gaze, her eyes wide. "How do you know? I have seen the ravages of disease here. People die a horrible, painful death." Her chest heaved with her sobs.

"Do you wish to leave here? Be with Leo?" Olivia whispered.

"Yes, but I fear I might have given him the disease. Now we will all die." Her voice held an edge of hysteria.

"Listen to me. We are going home. No one will die. Because no one is sick." Olivia sat up and stretched her arms to her side, palms up. "You see, there is naught wrong with me."

Maha's mouth dropped open in confusion. "But the physician just said…and you are covered in sores and you look terrible."

Olivia lifted a finger and ran it across one of the red spots on her chest. It smeared. "The physician said I would not die *here*. And I will not. Nor will you. We will go home and live long lives before we ever face that fate."

Maha looked at Olivia, her brow scrunched in confusion. "You are not sick?"

Olivia swiped at another spot on her chest. "No. It is paint." She quickly covered the smears with her shirt. "The sultan will wish us away, will he not?"

"Yes, yes!" Maha fell to her knees next to Olivia and took hold of her hand, kissing it. "Far away. As far as possible."

"But we must maintain this charade or who knows what will happen. You understand."

Maha nodded vigorously. "You are very sick and very contagious. And I have been with you, so I will most likely sicken, too. As will the ambassador and his men."

***

Tristan and Felix sat at a table in Tristan's apartment, playing chess and trying to work through various strategies to sway Moulay. There was whispering in the corridor and Tristan's first thought was the guards gossiped like a bunch of old women. But, what else did they have? Living in terror every day must be exhausting. Why, he and his men were worn down just from the limited number of days they had spent here. Yet there was something unusually frantic about the energy today.

Leo burst into the room and leaned down, hands on

his knees, to catch his breath. "Olivia has been sequestered into a small outbuilding. The physician came and went very quickly. Actually, in a matter of minutes."

"What does that mean?" Tristan wondered how he could determine her condition so quickly. Weren't there some kind of examinations required, some need to actually put hands on her? That could certainly not be accomplished in so short a time. What was amiss? Panic choked him. He tried to harness the heat rising in his chest. There had to be something he could do! He had enough of passivity. He needed to take some action to get to Olivia.

Leo dropped his head. "The guards say she is dying of some terrible disease."

"She what?" Tristan demanded. Olivia, dying? He had just seen her and she was well. Of course, he had heard of plagues that come quickly and take all the lives in their paths. No, this was too much to bear. He had to go to her. He ran from his room, the brothers tight on his heels.

The entire palace erupted into a frenzy. Men were running everywhere, some carrying bags filled with clothing, some with blankets and pillows. Men were shouting to one another and dashing in and out of apartments. Outside in the hallway was a chaos of motion. Tristan was determined to find Olivia and find out what was transpiring.

Before they could reach the end of the corridor, Tristan and his men were seized. They struggled but they were so outnumbered, resistance was futile. The three were dragged, still fighting, down the walkway and finally out into the courtyard. Here, too, men were racing about and shouting.

A cadre of soldiers was guarding the harem and

several women were escorted out. Tristan rose up on the balls of his feet to see if Olivia was among the group, but he saw nothing more than moving figures hidden behind veils. What was happening? And then, with terrible certainty, he knew. Plague. Of course, they were fleeing for their lives. But what if the guard was mistaken? What if Olivia was untouched by the disease? Would they force her to leave with the others?

The group hurried in the opposite direction and Tristan soon lost sight of them. He and the brothers were still being pulled forward to a cart. The three men were lifted and thrown onto the conveyance, which immediately set off at high speed. Tristan thought to jump out and follow the women, but he knew that would be foolish. Guards had confined the three into a tight knot, and they were totally surrounded.

The group of women had already out-distanced him and could not be reached. There was also the question of whether Olivia was even among those women at all. Would she be if she were truly ill? His chest tightened in frustration and he was nearly overcome with bloodlust. He wanted to kill every man who kept him from the woman he loved. And he would happily do so with his bare hands if necessary. He gritted his teeth, his heart hammered against his ribs. He'd find the opportunity.

Leo bellowed over the horses' hooves and the creaking of the cart. "We are headed for the wharf."

They were being evicted? Did the sultan think he could make a better bargain for Olivia? Did he think to keep her, after all? But that made no sense. And if she had been taken ill, how valuable would she be if she were dying? Tristan's head was about to explode from confusion and rage.

Clarity struck and he realized he had just spent time with her. If she was ill, or they believed it to be so, they would all think he might be tainted along with his men. He had to find Olivia.

The cart jarred to a halt at the waterfront. They were yanked from the back of the vehicle and pushed forward. One of the guards called out to an old boatman idling against a wooden post by the quay, cleaning his fingernails with a small blade.

"Take these men to their ship," the soldier demanded.

The boatman looked up, slightly disinterested.

"On pain of your death. By order of the Sultan Ismail Moulay."

This got the old man moving instantly. He jumped into his small rowboat and positioned it so the three could be shoved aboard. Two guards sprang in beside them, sword at the ready. They were all jostled into a sitting position and immediately the man started rowing toward the English vessel as if the dogs of hell were chasing him. Tristan exchanged looks with the brothers. They were as puzzled as he and gazed at him for their next move. Tristan had no intention of leaving this place without Olivia.

He contemplated diving off the rowboat as it pulled away from the wharf, but a glimmer of movement on the dock caught his eye. A group of soldiers were leading four bare-chested men carrying a litter as high above their heads as they could reach. Prone on top was a woman mostly concealed by a silken wrap that fell down the sides. Was she dead? Walking briskly next to her was the woman Maha and she looked very nervous. The woman on the bed had to be Olivia. Oh, dear God. He prayed she was alive.

Before Tristan and the others had reached their ship, another small boat sidled up to the quay. One of the guards pulled the small craft toward him and indicated the litter was to be lowered onto the vessel. It was too large to fit down inside the boat, so it extended precariously out across the sides. Tristan watched in horror as the boat rocked and swayed, the litter precariously close to being tossed into the water.

Tristan and his men were hastened up onto the deck of the ship and he watched in rapt attention as Maha carefully stepped into the other rowboat alongside the bed and tried valiantly to balance it to keep it from falling. Maha oddly did not seem the least bit distressed and it was confusing. *Did* Olivia occupy that bed? Were they sending her away to prevent more from becoming stricken with her illness? In a morose way, Tristan found consolation they would finally be reunited. If she was dying, he would comfort her and care for her and if he caught the plague, he cared not. He had no life without her.

The soldiers who had carried the litter backed away as the boatman pushed off, then they turned and disappeared. It seemed to Tristan as if they ran for their lives. Realization hit with the force of a blow. Olivia *was* on that bed and Maha was bringing her body to him. But how did it happen? Had she actually fallen ill or did the sultan kill her as an example and use the plague as an excuse so as not to raise the ire of the British monarchy? This was madness! He couldn't draw breath. *Olivia. Olivia.* He closed his eyes in utter despair. Not only had he failed to release her from the clutches of the monster, he had allowed her to die. He fell to his knees, his hands clasped before him, his head falling forward against the wooden side of the ship. A hand clutched his shoulder and he shook it off. He deserved no comfort.

154

"Tristan, she is not dead." Leo said it so gleefully, Tristan was surprised, but also encouraged.

"No?" A bright kernel of hope alit in his heart, but immediately sputtered out. "But she is dying, is she not?" His words held all the misery he felt.

"No. Not dying, either." Again, his tone was joyous.

Tristan gazed up at Leo. "How could you know that?" he demanded.

"Keep your head down," he snapped. "It will do no good to let on that we know."

"Know what?" Tristan snarled.

"Maha winked at me as the rowboat drew nearer. Something is happening and I can only think it is for the best."

"She winked at you?" The spark of optimism reignited.

"Maha. She winked to let me know it is not what it appears. But I believe you need to act as if Lady Olivia is lost to you. At least until we have set sail."

The old boatman bumped against the side of the ship and ropes were extended to the litter and wrapped around the poles. Carefully, it was lifted onto the deck. A rope ladder was extended to Maha, who wrapped it about her waist and allowed the men to pull her up. Once on the deck, she ran to Leo and threw her arms around his neck.

"Plague!" The shout from one of the crew rang out and vibrated about the ship and across the water.

"Plague!" shouted another, terror evident in his tone. "Let me off this ship!"

Tristan, Leo and Felix immediately reacted. They needed to quell panic. "Men, quiet! Why think you there is plague?"

"Look at her! She has the marks on her face." The

man was nearly hysterical. Several of the others starting shouting in their terror.

Tristan turned to see what was visible on Olivia's face. A corner of the veil had fallen away and the bright sunlight revealed red spots on her forehead and cheeks and her eyes bore deep smudges of grey beneath them. Indeed, she appeared she suffered from some dreadful disease.

The men, wide-eyed and slack jawed, backed to the far reaches of the vessel, desperate to put distance between them and get off the ship. Tristan held up his hand. "Wait! Listen to me. Even if that is the case, the sultan will not allow you back on shore. Do you not see the soldiers?"

A line of the sultan's men still stood on the dock, hands on swords, daring any of the ship's occupants to come ashore.

Tristan appealed to the captain. "Please ask your men to listen to me. I promise all will be well and no one will sicken."

"How could you know that?" the captain asked, his suspicious visible in his frown.

"Please captain, I beg you to trust me in this."

The captain hesitated a moment, then nodded.

Tristan gazed back at Olivia who opened her eyes and smiled at him. There was a glint of mischief in her gaze and he exhaled the terror that she had been lost to him. Her expression told him she was not near to death. The muscles in his chest eased and he found he could draw a deep breath again.

The captain stepped up onto a box and raised his hand to draw the attention of the crew.

"Listen to Lord Bathurst. I trust him and you must as well." The captain stood down and Tristan took his place.

"I promise you each an extra measure of gold and

double ration of rum if you will see to your work and set sail," Tristan announced. "The alternative is certain death," and he pointed to the dock.

The men, as one, lifted their gazes to the shore and saw the imminent threat there. Many dropped their heads, digesting Tristan's promise. Again, as one, they seemed to determine they had no choice. At least with the sickness, they had a chance. There was no doubt the waiting soldiers would cut them down if they tried to return to Morocco. Reluctantly, they moved away and started preparations to leave.

Tristan and the brothers maneuvered the litter across the deck with Maha following and eased it carefully down the flight of stairs and down the corridor to Tristan's cabin. Once inside, they were about to lay the bed down when Olivia threw off her covers, pulled off her veil and jumped off, laughing. She flung herself into Tristan's arms and kissed him soundly on the lips. He stepped back to look at her and gazed open-mouthed at the smeared paint on her face. Tentatively, he drew a finger across one of the marks, then gaped at his reddened fingertip. She nodded, grinning. "Makeup. All of it. I am quite well and finally safe from the horror that is that place. We are free!"

The ship lurched as it began to move out of its moorings and Tristan pulled her back into his arms. He was suffused with such joy and relief he could barely focus on her words. "I feared you were lost to me," he whispered.

"I, too, was fooled," Maha said. "I was certain she was dying. She did not tell me until after the physician confirmed her sickness," Maha explained. She leaned back against Leo, who wrapped his arms around her, his expression one of relief. Felix stood behind his brother, a hand on his shoulder.

Tristan frowned. "But why would the doctor do that? It would be dangerous for him to lie to Moulay."

Olivia smiled. "The pouch of gold you gave me was incentive and the doctor has no affection for the sultan. He knew we would be sent away immediately, so he would not be challenged in the lie."

Tristan finally understood. "All the flurry in the palace? They were all fleeing the plague."

"It seems the sultan fears naught but death. And sickness like the plague is not a pleasant or honorable way to die. So, he gathered his favorites and left," Maha informed them. "I had heard stories of this but had not seen it until this day. And he will be delighted we are gone from these shores. As are we all."

"You both are safe now," Leo said softly, gazing at Maha with adoration.

"I will not feel safe until we are far away from this place." But Tristan said this with a smile. "I must go back on deck and talk to the captain to see to our departure completed. I will return as quickly as I can." One more kiss and he and Leo left the cabin.

*** 

Olivia could not stop smiling. She twirled in a circle and wrapped her arms around herself. "We are free. We are free," she kept repeating, as if trying to actually believe it.

Maha clapped her hands in utter delight. "You kept your word. You saved me."

"Actually, it was Braheem. He came up with the plan and he knew you wanted to go."

Maha shook her head." There are no…"

"…secrets in the harem," Olivia finished for her and giggled.

"I shall serve you the rest of my days," Maha whispered, her head bowed.

"You will do no such thing. You will marry Leo and have lots of babies and live a happy life. No one deserves that more than you." Olivia stroked the other woman's arm.

"But how can I repay you?"

"You already have. You were my friend in a friendless place. I cannot tell you how much that meant to me."

"Is there naught I can do?" Maha brought her hands together in a gesture of prayer.

Olivia chewed her lower lip and smiled. "Actually, you can help me clean up the mess I have made with the kohl and paint."

Maha laughed out loud. "I wish all cures were so easy."

# Chapter Ten

The shore of Morocco quickly disappeared in the distance, like a nightmare fading upon awakening. Before them lay the open sea. The liberty was like the most delicious medicine, filling them all with joy. With the sultan believing Olivia had the plague, he would naturally assume she would kill all aboard. Perhaps he imagined the ship wandering about in the open sea forever, no crew, no passengers, no one. A ghost ship. A thing to be feared and never pursued. Which meant they were all finally free of Morocco.

Once they were clear of the land, and Olivia's skin was returned to its unpainted state, Tristan escorted her onto the deck. He wanted to reassure the captain and crew that she was not going to infect them. As they passed, the men gaped at her and audibly breathed their relief.

One man stepped forward. "We are so happy you are well, my lady," he said, bowing.

She gazed up to Tristan, grinning. "I am quite well. It seems it was only a rash or something equally non-threatening. Tell the others I am sorry if I worried them."

The man bowed again and scurried back to his post. But not before spreading the word. The tension left the deck like a weight being tossed overboard. A few of the men even began to sing.

160

The salty air washed over them like a cleansing bath. Tristan led Olivia to the railing and leaned back against it, pulling her between his legs. "Tell me everything that happened while you were there." There was obvious concern in his tone, and she reached up and put her palm against his cheek. He kissed it and gazed her directly in the eye. "Everything."

"There is really very little to tell. Looking back from the safety of this ship, I can say it was more of a learning experience than anything else. Morocco is a godforsaken place and the harem is like nothing I could have imagined. Even the stories my sisters related did not prepare me."

"No one harmed you?" he prodded.

"The sultan did not require my presence and most of the women either ignored me or tried to determine if I was their competition. With the exception of Maha. Although, her true name is Maggie. As I told you, her life story is one of great sadness and I am so happy she was able to come with us."

"I have no doubt Leo agrees." He smiled.

She cocked her head in question. "Who are they? Leo and the man with him?"

"They are brothers who have sworn fealty to my family for years. Felix is married, and I imagine Leo is soon to be in the same blessed state."

"I have no doubt my family will welcome you with open arms." He hoped that was true. He knew in his heart he wasn't the one to actually save her, so perhaps they would think him a failure and unworthy. He needed to prove he would spend the rest of his days protecting her and keeping her safe.

Olivia touched his cheek. "Tell me how this all came about. Your plan to rescue me."

He shook his head. "I failed, Olivia. I did not rescue you. This was the idea of another. It was the plague that allowed you to escape." He dropped his gaze, as if the wooden deck could offer refuge.

She placed her arms on his shoulders. "You came for me. You risked all and came for me. Do you not see that is enough? I would never have escaped without you."

Disappointment and shame dripped into his veins. "But I was not so wise as I imagined I would be. I had thought my cleverness would have the sultan in the palm of my hand. You could have paid the price for my inadequacies. I cannot think of the result had you not been *taken sick*."

"But we are here now. We are away from that terrible place and all the evil that abides there. That is what we must be grateful for. And you underestimate what you did. You showed amazing courage."

Olivia stepped back into a secluded space and pulled him with her. She leaned up on her toes and kissed him softly, then with hunger. He parted her lips with his tongue and her mouth opened, her tongue mating with his. He was unapologetic how his desire for her was evident as she pressed her body closer.

Breathless from need, he pulled back. "I want to make love to you. I am burning with it. But I will not ruin your reputation. We must speak the vows." He desperately wanted her as his wife, as much as he desired to have her cry out his name beneath him. He wanted to fall asleep each night with her beside him and awaken each morning with her in his arms for the rest of their lives. He prayed she felt the same.

Olivia inhaled, then slowly blew out her breath. "It is weeks until we reach home." She sounded as if she wanted to cry and he, too, dreaded the long trip home.

An idea took shape. "We could handfast."

"Handfast? I have heard of such a thing, but I do not know how it comes about. It is as valid as the words spoken by a priest?"

"It is. We could have witnesses who would attest to the lawful nature of it. And have a more official ceremony later."

Olivia clapped her hands together. "When?"

"So you will?" Light filled his heart. He was over the moon with joy. She was to be his wife!

"With all my heart. Just tell me when."

"On the morrow. Here, on the deck. What say you?" She hesitated and a frisson of fear crawled up his spine.

"What of Leo and Maggie? Could they marry, as well?"

Relief was like a cool breeze and he shrugged. "I do not see why not, if that is their wish." Of course she would think of others. It was one of the things he so loved about her.

"I will ask Maggie, and you ask Leo. And I must make preparations. I am to be a bride." And she danced away, her hands high in the air. As he watched her go, he knew he was the most blessed among men.

\*\*\*

Dinner in the galley that night was a happy affair. The food was bland compared to that they had eaten in Morocco, but so much more delicious since it was consumed here together and free. Tristan and Olivia sat so close together on the wooden bench they were as one. She was content for the first time in weeks. Release from the tyranny of the devil could do that.

163

Her thoughts were filled with her love for Tristan and plans for the morrow. She was to be his wife and she could barely contain her excitement. Maggie sat across from her, gazing at Leo as if he were the moon in the heavens. Felix just shook his head and grinned.

Wine was poured, and the mood was jovial. Leo lifted his glass. "My lady, Olivia, you are looking quite well after that terrible siege of plague. I am pleased you have recovered." He held up his glass. "To the women who survived and to the men who will now receive the greatest of gifts. To true love."

"And to the men who came for us, despite the dangers, Olivia added.

She leaned in and kissed Tristan soundly on the mouth. Leo, following her lead, kissed

Maggie. Then, they all dissolved into laughter.

Soon, exhaustion from all they had suffered seeped into the celebration, weighing heavily upon Olivia's eyelids. The entire company was tired, and it was time for sleep.

"Maggie and I shall spend the night together," she announced, "since we need to preserve our virtue." Her tone was mischievous.

Both Tristan and Leo groaned, and the women giggled.

"Which means we men must sleep in the hold, since there are but two cabins on this vessel," Tristan groused, but the women ignored him.

Olivia held out her hand to Maggie and they wandered out of the galley and down the corridor to Tristan's cabin.

"What shall we wear tomorrow?" Maggie's voice trembled with anticipation.

"Well," Olivia laughed, "I still have several scarves

left over from the *babe* I carried. Perhaps we can use them to add some more style to our garments."

Maggie squeezed her hands together in delight. "Tomorrow night we will be wed to the men we love. We will be wives."

A soothing wash flowed through Olivia. All things happened for a reason and as terrible as her experience in Morocco had been, it was all worth it to come to this. She was about to marry Tristan, Maggie was saved and had a chance at happiness, as well, and she had gained a close friend who was bound to her by their experiences.

Olivia had no sooner slipped under the covers on her cot when sleep claimed her. She was locked in a cage, with a devil tormenting her. The thing lashed out, cutting her skin and screeching at her. She was desperately trying to find a means to get out, but the demon just continued its assault. She thrashed about, fighting back, but she was weakening and losing the battle. The thing was going to overpower her, and she would die.

An agonizing foreign sound ripped from her throat. Olivia bolted upright, soaked in perspiration. Tears dripped down her cheeks. And then Tristan was beside her, speaking unintelligible words that calmed. The dream lost its grip and she blinked at him.

"You had a nightmare." He stroked her hair, holding her tight to soothe her. A sob broke from her chest. "It was terrible," she whispered. She could not speak of it, for fear it might become real.

"It was just a bad dream. You are here with me and you are safe," he said, stroking her back.

"I woke you?"

"I believe you woke the entire vessel." He laughed, but his words were not chastising.

Her blush warmed her cheeks. "I am so sorry. Forgive me."

"There is naught to forgive. You have been through hell. The memories will not just go quickly."

Moonlight poured in through the porthole above them and she could see the adoration for her in his eyes.

"I love you, Tristan."

"And I you." He kissed her softly and then peered across to the makeshift cot on the other side of the space. "Where is Maggie?"

Olivia peered over his shoulder. "I must have awakened her. Perhaps she went up for some air. I am so sorry I have disrupted everyone's night."

"Shush now and rest. I will go find her. Tomorrow promises to be a very special day." She was concerned for Maggie, but more, she was excited to be married at the same time as her friend,

Olivia had just settled back into her bed when the cabin door was thrown open. Leo carried Maggie while Tristan stepped in behind him and lit a lamp. Blood streaked her face and her cheeks had drained of all color. Olivia scurried from her cot and ran to her friend, then turned terrified to Tristan. "What happened?"

Stricken, Leo said, "She must have fallen. There is blood everywhere." His breath hitched, but he continued. "I couldn't sleep, and I went up on deck. I saw her crumpled in a corner. Will she live?" He had paled considerably and looked like he was going to be sick.

"Where was the night watchman?" Tristan asked.

"On the other side of the ship." Leo shook his head in frustration. "I called for the surgeon."

"She will be fine." Olivia hoped her words would come to fruition.

A moment later a knock sounded and a man of about forty years entered. He marched over to Maggie and quickly assessed her. Very gently, the man pulled back her friend's hair to reveal a gash on the side of her forehead.

His years spent at sea had turned his skin dark, but the wrinkles when he smiled at them was reassuring. "It looks worse than it is," he said. "The head tends to bleed a lot." I will need some linen and some water."

Olivia scurried to tear a piece of sheet from the bed while Tristan grabbed the basin that had been filled with water earlier. They handed both to the doctor.

"Bring the lamp closer," he asked Tristan.

Carefully, the man bathed Maggie's face and then pressed the cloth on the wound. Maggie groaned and her eyes fluttered open.

"What happened?" She was bleary-eyed but conscious now.

"We were hoping you could tell us," Tristan said.

"Are you all right?" Leo stroked her arm, exhaling his relief that she was awake.

"I…I don't know." Groggy, her words were thick. "I remember I was too excited to sleep, so I went up on deck. I should have remembered I was no longer in the harem, protected by the eunuchs. I heard a scream and when I realized it had to be Olivia, I ran toward the stairs to return to the cabin. Then, I was hit, I think from the side."

"I am so sorry. I screamed because I had a nightmare. But, hit? By something? Someone?" Olivia frowned. "Perhaps the ship rolled and knocked you off balance?"

"I don't know. I could have walked into something I suppose. It was dark. And I was moving fast." She shook her head as if to clear it and blinked in pain.

Olivia turned to Tristan. "No one in the crew would do this, would they?"

167

He shook his head. "There would be no reason."

Leo's color rose. "It had better not have been anyone aboard."

The physician released his pressure on wound and it still bled. "Can one of you tear off some more strips from the sheet. Then wet one in the basin and bring them all to me."

Leo jumped up, obviously happy to be able to do something useful.

After a few minutes, the bleeding had stopped, and Maggie was able to sit up. Leo sat behind her and held onto her shoulders to brace her. She leaned back against him, more relaxed now. "How do you feel?" the doctor asked.

"Clumsy. I must have bumped into something in my haste. My head hurts, but I will be all right."

"Then I will go. If it bleeds again, please call me," he said and left the cabin.

"I was so worried," Leo said, kissing her on the cheek.

"You worry too much," she teased.

"When it comes to you, I cannot worry enough."

"Do you think you can sleep now?" Olivia asked her softly.

"I think so. We do not wish to have dark circles under our eyes for tomorrow, do we?" Maggie was trying to lighten the mood.

Olivia gave a quick shrug of her shoulders. "No. We do not. I am just grateful you were not hurt worse."

"As are we all." Leo placed another kiss on Maggie's cheek. Reluctantly, he stood and both men left the cabin.

"What really happened?" Olivia asked, when the men had gone.

"It is as I said. I think I just hit something as I was running back to the cabin. It is the only explanation."

"You saw no one?" Olivia prodded.

"No. I was alone. Or I think so. But...no, I am certain it was my own awkwardness."

Olivia sighed her relief. She did not wish to worry that the devil would be coming for them. Or that one of the crewman was malicious. They had only just escaped from those that would do them harm. The thought of one of the sultan's evil minions here was too much to bear.

"Let's get some sleep," Olivia said, climbing back into her bed and dozed. In what seemed like a mere minute or two, daylight was streaming through the window and morning had arrived. She looked over to Maggie, who was sleeping peacefully. Quietly, she slipped out of bed and to check the other woman. A large, dark bruise stood out against the white skin of her forehead on the right side. Again, a frisson of fear coursed up Olivia's spine. What if someone had sneaked aboard that wanted to hurt them? No. She tamped down the possibility. She had spent too many weeks in constant trepidation. Today was to be her wedding day and she made up her mind to banish any bad thoughts.

Maggie opened her eyes and smiled. Gingerly, she touched the lump on her head. "Does it look terrible?"

"We can comb your hair so it does not show at all," Olivia reassured her. "How do you feel?"

"I do have a slight headache, but it will not interfere with today." She grinned. "We are getting married."

"Yes, we are!" And Olivia spun about the tiny room, giggling with pure joy.

\*\*\*

Tristan, Leo and Felix stood at the stern, waiting for the women and the handfasting to begin. Nerves tightened Tristan's muscles and his legs twitched. He couldn't remember when he had been more excited. Tonight, Olivia would be his forever and he would make love to her until they both collapsed from exhaustion. The thought made him grin.

"Thinking of later?" Felix asked.

"How did you know?" Tristan was surprised at his perception.

"You forget, I have been a bridegroom." He nodded knowingly.

"Ah, and I shall not forget to remind your wife of your loyalty as a husband, even when tempted by beautiful women." Tristan raised an eyebrow.

"Perhaps neither of you should mention the women," Felix responded. "It is never good to tempt fate."

Leo laughed. "Perhaps," he agreed.

"Nervous?" Leo asked Tristan.

"Not at all. You?" The shaking of his hands belied his comment.

"Of course not."

"You are both such terrible liars," Felix mocked. "It will all be over in a trice and you can get to the important matters."

"The important matters," both Tristan and Leo said in unison and then laughed.

It was then the women appeared. Tristan's breath caught in his throat and his heart threw itself into his ribs. She was a vision. An angel. The sunlight painted her hair with shimmering light and her dark eyes warmed to deep pools of promise as she glided to him. He barely noticed Maggie was next to her, but he was certain Leo was as transfixed by his bride as Tristan was with his.

He stretched out his hand to her and she floated to him. They stood facing each other, their gazes locked in an embrace of love.

Felix stepped up beside them and nodded. Tristan soaked in the beautiful woman before him and his lips lifted in a gentle smile.

"Olivia, I have loved you since the first time I set eyes upon you. I would go to the ends of the earth, battle dragons, fight demons, to claim you as mine. And now, today, you are here, and I promise to love you forever and always protect and care for you. We will explore whatever life presents and we will do it as one. I will love you, always."

She clasped his hands tighter. "Tristan, I have loved you since the first time I set eyes upon you. You have already proven your words, since you have gone to the ends of the earth and battled demons for me. And I promise to choose you always and stand by your side, no matter what comes. I will love you forever." A tear trickled down her cheek and she smiled at him with so much love, his heart ached with stretching, it was so full.

Then, Felix stepped closer and tied their wrists together with a soft piece of cord. "And so you have bound yourselves together forever, just as this rope binds you now."

Felix took a step back and Tristan pressed his lips to hers, pouring out all the emotion he felt. The pressure both burned and caressed and he was more content and happier than he had ever been in his life.

The two, still tied together, turned and listened as Leo and Maggie recited their promises to each other. Their hands were tied and Leo kissed his bride. A cheer from the crew rang out and danced across the waves.

# Chapter Eleven

The four had eaten their fill and sipped wine and bathed in the joy of both freedom and new commitment. Leo and Maggie drifted away, and Tristan held out his hand to his new bride. They strolled down the corridor to his cabin and Tristan closed the door, wrapping them in the quiet. Tristan lit a lamp and suddenly Olivia was beset with trembling that started in her stomach and fluttered throughout her body. It was as if a mass of butterflies had taken hold of her insides.

Tristan sensed her nerves. He vibrated, too. "I love you, Olivia," he said.

"Oh, and I love you, Tristan." She took a step back and dropped her gaze.

"Then what is it?" But she was apprehensive about discovering her womanhood on an intimate level and didn't know what to do. As if he understood her reluctance, he reached out and stroked her arm. "I love you, Olivia," he repeated. "And that means I would never hurt you."

She nodded and knew in her deepest heart that what he said was true. She trusted this man with her life, with her very soul, and she walked forward into his arms. He held her and whispered into her hair. The words were so quiet, she could not discern what he said, but she knew in

172

her heart what he meant. She turned her face up to him and he lowered his mouth to hers. The kiss was soft, flesh against delicate flesh. His tongue traced her lower lip and her mouth opened to receive it. The kiss deepened and the butterflies flew away, replaced with a wave of fire that coursed through her, hot and full of need.

He opened her top and slipped it from her shoulders as his hand cupped her breast. His thumb teased the nipple until it was tight. Her breathing became rapid and she straightened her back, pushing closer to give him greater access. He bent and took the hard nub in his mouth, and Olivia thought she would lose her mind with the pleasure. He shifted to the other breast and her knees weakened.

He gripped her hips and lifted her. Instinctively, her legs wrapped around his waist, her needy core throbbing with demand. He carried her to the bed and placed her back onto the soft counterpane. She stretched out as he pulled off her slippers and released the belt that held up her pants. He eased them down her legs and, now she was bare to him. She had never been naked in front of a man before and she had to fight her natural modesty. This was Tristan, the man she loved and she longed to give him everything. The appreciative look in his eyes emboldened her.

He kissed her ankles, her knees, her thighs. His tongue left a molten path as he inched with agonizing slowness to the part of her aching for attention. Her eyes were shut tight in anticipation. And then he was between her legs, sucking on her softness, stoking and fanning flames never before ignited. She wrapped her fists in the sheets and her heart pounded, her blood soaring through her veins. She focused on the magic of his mouth on her, the pressure building, until she was flying heavenward, the stars fulfilling a promise she was unaware they had made.

She floated back to earth, breathless, amazed, enthralled. She lifted her arms to him, beckoning him to mount her, and he quickly stripped off his clothes and laid down beside her. She had never seen a nude man before and the sight of his hard-muscled body made her desire him all the more. She desperately wanted to explore the angles and planes of him. Olivia slid her hands along down to his hips and, summoning courage, wrapped her hand around his manhood. He sharply inhaled through his teeth in pleasure and she smiled, then angled her head to him.

"I will be gentle," he reassured her. "I have been told it will hurt at first."

"I am ready," she said, pulling him closer.

He braced himself on his forearms and guided into her. She felt the guardian resist, then a quick, sharp jab of pain and Tristan ceased his movement. But, as quickly as it happened, it was replaced with the throbbing desire. She raised her hips to encourage him and he sank deep inside her. She could feel her insides welcoming him, and he began to move, very slowly at first, then faster.

The blazing in her core was all-consuming and, when she thought she could go no higher without being completely consumed, she exploded into a fever of light as he called out her name in his own release.

He dropped down beside her and kissed her. "Are you all right?"

"No, I am so much better than that. If I had only known, I would have insisted you take me in the woods months ago."

He opened his mouth in mock surprise. "My wife is a brazen hussy." He grinned.

She grinned in return. "And you are most welcome."

*Freed From Morocco*

She turned innocent eyes to him. "I think we should do it again."

"As I said—brazen. And yes, I am a lucky man. But you will be sore. So try to behave until you have healed."

She feigned a pout. "And how long should that take?"

"For you, probably a few hours," he said and touched the tip of her nose with his fingertip. "Now go to sleep, wife. It has been a very busy few days and I have no doubt you are exhausted."

She heaved a sigh. "Oh, I don't know. Don't most people contract the plague, escape from captivity, recover and then get married all in the span of two days?"

"Not most people," he retorted gleefully.

She enjoyed their light-hearted banter, but sleep wrapped her up tightly in its warm embrace.

Olivia was awakened a few hours later by a woman's scream. This time she was not the one calling out. Tristan was already pulling on his pants before she could fathom what was happening.

He ran from the cabin and Olivia quickly donned her garments and followed him. What she saw on deck stopped her in her tracks. Amelia sat in a huddled bundle, shivering and crying, surrounded by several of the crewmen who looked either bewildered or unnerved or both. One man had brought a blanket to cover her.

"Amelia?" Olivia rushed over to the woman. Amelia looked up and tears poured down her face. Her lips quivered and her face was swollen from crying.

"You know her?" Tristan asked.

"Her sister was the one who was…"

She didn't need to finish her sentence. Tristan nodded in understanding.

175

Felix, Leo, and Maggie had joined them, and they all stared at Amelia as if she were an apparition.

"How did you get here, Amelia?" Olivia frowned, confused.

"I…I…I…Jaffar…" She broke off into sobs.

"Jaffar?" Tristan turned to Olivia.

"He is the head eunuch." She shook her head, thoroughly baffled now. "Is Jaffar with you?"

"He…was. He fell." Amelia dropped her head into her hands.

"Fell where?" Tristan prodded.

The captain stepped forward. "Overboard, my lord."

"What?" Tristan demanded of the man.

"We heard a scream," a crewman said. The lady was leaning over the railing. We feared for her, so we grabbed her back, but she said there was a man in the water. We saw no one." The man looked around and several of the other nodded their agreement. "She called for him, but there was no response."

"Are you certain you could not save him?" the captain addressed the men.

"We saw no one in the water, sir. He must have gone down as soon as he hit the water. Could have broken his neck. We watched and called out, but there was nothing." This from a third crewman.

"And no one saw him fall?" the captain demanded.

"I was on watch, sir. It was dark and I wasn't looking on the deck. I was looking out to sea," the man explained.

The captain nodded his acceptance and turned to Tristan. "I am sorry, my lord."

"Let's get her to the galley. She looks as if she could use some rum. And we need some answers." Tristan was clearly not satisfied by the explanation of what had transpired. Leo and Felix stepped up to help her, but Maggie hung back.

"I don't trust her," Maggie hissed in Olivia's ear.

"Nor I," Olivia answered. A bad feeling swept through her. Had she brought trouble aboard this ship? She, too, wanted some clarification. "But we should hear her story." Anxious to hear more, she and Maggie followed the others below.

Once settled into a chair covered with another blanket and sipping from a cup of rum, Amelia lost her pinched expression and her tears had ceased.

"Amelia. What happened to Jaffar?" This from Olivia. "And how did you get here?" She had to work to keep the suspicion from her tone.

Amelia sniffed once and straightened. "He helped me. When all were running away, I was certain your ship would be sent back to England. I was desperate to get home. You understand," she appealed to Olivia.

"Go on," Tristan urged when Amelia hesitated.

"Jaffar agreed to help me. During all the chaos at the palace, he showed me the way to the dock and secured a small boat. He rowed to the ship, but I was frightened and worried we would be discovered, and, if something went amiss, captured and returned. So, we hid below in the front section of the cargo hold. I didn't want him to accompany me, but he insisted."

By now, Amelia was out of breath and paused to take a deep draught of her rum. She snuggled deeper into the blanket.

"Go on, Amelia," Olivia prodded.

"Wait, you are not ill?" Amelia tilted her head, confused.

"I am quite recovered, thank you," Olivia responded.

177

"So it was a ruse?" There was a sneer underlying her tone. "You are more clever than I thought."

Olivia suppressed the urge to slap the woman. Instead, Olivia pasted a smile upon her face. "Your story?" she urged. "Please continue."

"Well, we waited until we were certain the ship would not be detained or return to port. So, tonight…I was so hungry, you see…"

Amelia was clearly aware all eyes were on her, and she seemed to preen with the attention. Olivia was again struck by the woman's arrogance. A man had just died, a man who loved her and protected her, and she was more concerned with holding her audience rapt. Olivia closed her eyes and prayed for patience.

When Amelia didn't pick up her tale again, Tristan huffed. "Do tell us more."

"Oh, yes," she continued, "I wanted something to eat and drink. We had been in that hole for days and I was weak. So Jaffar sneaked upon deck in search of some nourishment. It wasn't so easy for him, you know. He was very large."

Forcing the rest of her story was nerve-racking.

"Yes…" Felix encouraged.

Amelia looked at him, her eyes wide. "And who are you?" she demanded, scowling.

Tristan waved his hand to the brothers and introduced them, and then Amelia turned her disdainful gaze to Maggie. "I know you. Maha. You are a servant. Why are you here?"

Leo stepped forward, fire in his eyes. "This is my wife and her name is Maggie."

Amelia flicked her wrist. "Of course she is." She expelled a breath. "Anyway, I grew tired of waiting for Jaffar and just as I came up on deck to look for him, I saw him fall into the water. That's when I screamed." She swallowed another sip from her cup. "Is there anything to eat. I am half-starved."

His disgust evident, Felix rooted around in the nearest cupboard and produced a loaf of stale bread. He held it out to her. She sneered, but grabbed it from him, broke off a piece, and proceeded to cram it into her mouth.

When Amelia had managed most of the food, she sat back and yawned widely. "I have had a terrible ordeal. First, all that I suffered in Morocco and losing my sister and all. And then everything else. I am exhausted. Will someone show me to my cabin?"

Olivia could not help but be amazed at the woman's arrogance. Amelia was aware only of her own discomfort and cared naught for the others here who had suffered as well.

"Well," said the captain, stepping forward. We do not have passenger cabins. We can make a bed for you in one of the storage rooms." He strode from the room, presumably to give the order.

Amelia's eyes widened. "No cabin?" But she seemed to immediately realize she was on precarious ground and dropped her gaze. "I suppose that will be an improvement over the cargo hold." The sneer was obvious.

"Felix, please escort Amelia to her sleeping quarters," Tristan directed.

All eyes went to Felix, who glared back at them. He tilted his head and Amelia slowly rose and followed him. "I trust there will be more for breakfast on the morrow," she said loftily as she left the room. The others gave a collective sigh.

"It appears it is going to be a very long voyage home," Leo said as they filed out of the galley.

\*\*\*

Tristan and Olivia had just settled in their cabin with Leo and Maggie when Maggie sighed loudly.

"What is it?" Olivia asked.

"She is lying," Maggie stated flatly. Leo was standing behind his wife and wrapped his arms around her shoulders. "I think she is the one who shoved me when I was on deck, hoping I would fall, and I think she pushed Jaffar into the sea."

Tristan was stunned. "Why would you make such an accusation?"

"Because she lies," Olivia said. "Jaffar was in love with her and I believe he would have done anything she asked. And she used him to her own ends."

Tristan looked at her, his eyes wide in question. She related Amelia's behavior from when she first met the girl up until the incident she had witnessed in the garden. "And she asked Jaffar to go to the sultan and tell him I was not with child."

"Yes," Maggie affirmed. "I know that to be true. Everyone in the harem knew she was dangerous. And she pushed Olivia into a fountain."

"She did what?" Tristan demanded.

"It is not important now," Olivia soothed. "It was nothing."

Tristan ran his hand along the back of his neck. "Then I am unsure what to do. Going back is out of the question and in all good conscience, we cannot leave her ashore in a foreign land. Perhaps she felt desperate and hoped to save herself."

"Jaffar is dead." Leo said. "How do you imagine it happened?" His tone suggested he was more than suspicious.

"It could have been an accident," Tristan replied. "If he was such a large man, perhaps he was awkward. He might have tripped on some rope and toppled overboard.."

"Why do you defend her," Olivia asked, anger coiling. Amelia had been naught but a problem since the beginning.

"I am not defending her," he said. "I just think she might not be as terrible as you all think."

Now, Olivia was boiling mad. He was defending her and Amelia didn't deserve it.

"And, even if she is, we must get her back to English shores. It is the only honorable thing to do."

Of course he was right. But the thought of weeks with Amelia on their ship set Olivia's teeth on edge. Perhaps Amelia was not as bad as they feared, but she was not pleasant company. Olivia recalled all too vividly the constant whining on the trip to Morocco. Olivia inwardly groaned. If it had to be endured, at least Tristan and her new friends were there to offer a diversion.

After Leo and Maggie left, Tristan opened his arms and Olivia snuggled against him, relishing the feel of him. Loving him was the only emotion she would allow herself tonight.

\*\*\*

Breakfast was as annoying as they all imagined it would be. Amelia did naught but complain.

"Is there not a cabin?" she asked, not bothering with a morning greeting.

"No. This ship was built for cargo, not passengers," Tristan responded.

"Well, why did you not hire a passenger ship?" she asked, her tone petulant.

"This was the vessel that was available," he explained, more calmly than Olivia would have.

"Well, can we at least put into port so I can buy some new clothes? These are so—uncivilized." She swept her hand down her body to emphasize her statement.

"I don't know about you, Amelia, but I am most anxious to return home. As are the rest of us," Olivia said with feigned patience and the others nodded their affirmation.

Amelia huffed and shoved another slice of buttered bread into her mouth. "Have you no fresh meat aboard?"

This last was ignored. The remainder of the meal continued to be unpleasant, the tension thick enough to cut with a knife.

Later, when they were walking hand in hand on deck, Tristan turned to Olivia. "You know, I have been thinking. Perhaps that is not such a terrible suggestion."

Olivia frowned, puzzled. "Which suggestion was that?"

"Perhaps we might put into port in Portugal for a day or so. You could all get some proper clothes and we could take a tour of the city. After all you have suffered, it might be nice to have a holiday of sorts."

The idea was tempting, but the idea that Tristan was pandering to Amelia infuriated her. Did he find the woman attractive? She forced herself to tamp down her jealousy.

"You are certain my family is well?" she asked, pointedly.

He smiled his assurance. "I know you would like to see them as soon as possible, but a day's delay should not matter much, and it might help put the past behind us."

"How far away are we? From the port, I mean?"

He pointed to a strip of land jutting out to the right.

"Spain is there. Portugal is up the coast, but we should be able to reach it in a day or so."

"So we are already in another country?" Olivia was delighted.

He nodded. We could take a day and take on some fresh food and supplies. It will make the journey home more pleasant. And I am certain you would be pleased with a new gown or two."

Olivia pressed her lips together, barely containing her excitement. "It would almost be like a honeymoon."

"So you agree it is a sound idea? Because when Amelia suggested it—"

"I am afraid anything she says comes out as a grievance. I don't trust her, Tristan. I have seen how she can manipulate others." And she didn't like it when he spoke of the woman.

"Did you consider it might have been the situation?" He lifted a brow. "Her sister was brutally murdered, and she does not strike me as one with a strong constitution."

It bothered her that Tristan defended the other woman, but she had no wish to create an issue by disagreeing. It would serve naught. "To answer your question, I think stopping for a day or so would be a wonderful idea," she said and kissed him.

"Then I shall speak with the captain. I have no doubt the crew will also be pleased to have some time off this vessel."

He strode away and Olivia leaned back against the railing. She was enjoying the salty breeze when she heard footsteps. Her joy turned to irritation when she saw it was Amelia who approached.

"Olivia. A word?" A half-smile lifted her lips.

"Of course, Amelia." She gritted her teeth in anticipation of whatever complaint Amelia intended to lodge.

183

"I want to apologize. I wasn't very nice to you and I am truly sorry." She placed a hand over her heart. "But I was so frightened and when Charlotte—well, you know—I just seemed to lose my mind."

Olivia doubted the other woman's sincerity. All her instincts told her Amelia was not to be trusted.

"I understand." *Keep your friends close...*

"I just passed Tristan and he said we would be landing in Spain for a day or so. I am very delighted. I am certain you would like some new gowns, as would I. I assume Maha, or whatever her name is, will remain on the ship. That is the place of servants, is it not?"

Outrage pushed blood into Olivia's cheeks and tensed her every muscle. "Maggie is not a servant. She was kidnapped, no different than you or I."

"Oh please, Olivia. She is not one of us. She is not of the nobility." She lifted her shoulder in emphasis.

Olivia wanted nothing more than to punch her in her supercilious expression. Instead, she knotted her fists at her sides.

"Maggie is my friend and will be treated accordingly." The words were spoken slowly for effect and Amelia responded with a patient smile.

"Of course. That's what I meant. Noblesse oblige."

Olivia could no longer contain her temper, so she walked away from the other woman rather than give into the temptation to wipe the feigned smile off her face. Olivia realized she had never in her life met someone she actually detested until now. She told herself to just stay as far from Amelia as possible, which was not an easy task on a ship. But soon they would be on land and she could claim at least some respite.

# Chapter Twelve

Portugal was a magical land. John and Shera had spent some time here when they left Morocco, too, but their descriptions did not do it justice. Olivia was captivated. She and Tristan decided to go exploring by themselves.

The architecture was intricate and magnificent, and the people were warm and welcoming. The houses were set in a maze of earthen tones, their red roofs gleaming in the daylight. Everywhere they went, locals smiled and looked genuinely pleased to see them. They wandered through a marketplace and Tristan had her wait under a tree while he disappeared into the crowd. He returned a few minutes later bearing a small velvet bag.

Delighted, she opened it and saw a beautifully wrought hammered gold wedding band. She held it up to the sunlight and it sparkled as it reflected the rays. "It's gorgeous," she exclaimed. She thought she'd never be this happy again and she was going to cherish every moment. And this man who brought her so much joy.

He slipped it onto her finger and kissed her knuckles. "You had no wedding band. And now you do," he whispered. "When we return home, I will replace it with my grandmother's ring."

"I love this one. I will wear it always," she promised.

They purchased a dress that was similar in style and cut to an English gown. It was a deep crimson and it glowed against her olive skin. "You look even more beautiful," Tristan exclaimed, and her cheeks warmed with pleasure.

Tired from shopping, they rested at an outdoor café. Olivia remembered John saying Portugal was known for its fine wines and he was so right. They sat in the shade and held hands, savoring their drinks, just content to be together.

"We should go back to the ship," Tristan said after a while.

She sighed. "I wish we could stay here forever."

"No you don't. You'd miss your family too much," he teased.

"You're right. I cannot wait to see them and ease their minds. They must imagine terrible things have transpired."

"I promised them I would find you and bring you home."

"And you are keeping your vow." She leaned over to kiss him softly.

Tristan cupped the nape of her neck and deepened the kiss. "We should go back now," he declared after breaking away, clearing his throat.

They gathered their purchases and hurried back to the dock. The ship rode the harbor like the sanctuary it had become. They boarded and, seeing naught was amiss, made their way quickly to their cabin.

When they emerged an hour later, one of the crew approached Tristan. "We are ready to go as soon as the tide cooperates," the man declared.

"All are back on board?" Tristan asked.

"Yes, sir."

Amelia came strolling across the deck in a proper English gown. Her gaze was focused on Tristan, but she seemed to sense the crewmen gawking at her. She was preening and Olivia bit down on her back teeth. When she reached Olivia and Tristan she spun around. "How do I look?"

"Lovely," he exclaimed, a little too enthusiastically, and Olivia's stomach clenched. She chastised herself; he was only being polite, after all.

"How did you manage to get a corset?" Olivia asked.

Amelia smiled. "With enough incentive, anyone can get anything."

A chill crawled up Olivia's spine.

\*\*\*

They set sail on the tide before first light and it was comforting to lay in Tristan's arms, the gentle rocking of the ship soothing. They had just made love and Olivia should have been completely content, but something had been bothering her. Suddenly, she finally was able to understand what it was.

"How did she pay?" she asked without preamble.

"How did who pay what?" Tristan asked.

"Amelia. How did she pay for the gown and the corset?" Olivia could find no rational explanation.

Tristan frowned. "I have no idea. Why do you concern yourself?"

"Do you not wonder how she came into possession of coin?" she prodded, wondering if Tristan may have given her some.

He shrugged. "No. It is a fair question, but it is none

of my concern. Maybe one of the crewmen took pity on her." He stroked her hair and held her closer. "You have spent too much time around evil people. Not everyone has malevolent intent."

"I suppose you're right. It's just—I saw her play the part of a crazy woman with Jaffar, when she was just using him."

"Olivia, my love, people will go to great extremes to survive. Perhaps that was just the choice she made." He sounded so reasonable and he was probably right.. "Now come closer and kiss me."

"With pleasure, my love."

***

The days were spent watching the land speed by, although not fast enough for Olivia's taste. They all walked on the deck, took their meals together and tried to think up ways to make the time pass more quickly.

One afternoon, Maggie asked one of the crew to set a stick upright in the bow. She had fashioned some rings out of rope, and she called the group together.

"I am going to teach you quoits," she announced. "It is a Scottish pub game."

All were interested in anything that would occupy their time.

"How does it work?" Leo asked.

She held up the rings she had fashioned. "We throw these to that stick over there. The object is to get the ring over the spike or as near to it as possible."

"Is there a prize for the winner?" Leo leered at her.

"I hadn't thought of that," she responded, pouting in disappointment.

"Playing is the prize." Olivia reached for one of the hoops of rope.

Amelia looked at them and raised her chin. "Well, I think it a waste of time. So…plebian."

"Do you have a better way to occupy our time?" Maggie asked, pressing her lips together.

Amelia turned on her heel and stomped down the deck.

The others ignored her and spent a few happy hours play-fighting over whose ring was closer.

\*\*\*

The captain approached Tristan on the deck later that afternoon. "My lord, I have a question."

"Of course," Tristan encouraged him.

"The cook has asked if there is a reason his bread and dried meats keep disappearing from the pantry."

Tristan frowned. "Is he certain?"

"Yes, my lord. I have known the man for years and it is not like him to complain without reason."

"Do you think the crew is undernourished?" Tristan was definitely concerned.

"Oh, no, my lord. They are eating better on this ship than they ever have. You were most generous when you stocked the galley."

"So they would have no reason to pilfer food?" This was confusing. "How much is missing?"

"Enough to sustain a large man. And it has been happening since we left Morocco." He hesitated a moment and stood straighter. "My lord, we may be sailors, but we are men of honor. No one believes themselves better than another on this vessel and stealing is a punishable offense."

"So you believe there is reason for suspicion," Tristan asked.

"I do, my lord. We have searched the ship, and found naught, but I thought I should warn you. There might be another stowaway that has managed to elude us."

"Thank you, Captain. I will alert my men and we will maintain vigilance."

The captain's information weighed on Tristan as he made his way back to his cabin. His mood immediately lightened when he saw there was a woman in his bed. His wife was insatiable and he could not have been more delighted. He quickly stripped off his clothes and pulled back the covers.

Shock froze him in place. It was not his beloved Olivia laying naked on the cot. Amelia smiled at him seductively.

He backed away, his surprise quickly turning to anger. "What are you doing?" he demanded.

She cocked her head suggestively. "What does it look like?" she said, skimming her hand across her bare breast.

"Get dressed and get out of my cabin," he growled. He grabbed his pants and was pulling them on just as the door opened. Olivia's mouth dropped open and the blood drained from her cheeks. His stomach dropped, knowing how this must look to his wife. Guilt pressed in on him, even though he had done nothing wrong. Olivia took a step back, closed the door, and he could hear her footsteps retreating.

He turned back to Amelia, the fury coursing through him like burning coals. Rage at how Amelia had set him up nearly choked him. It was all he could do not to choke the woman. Because of her, he had hurt Olivia. "Get. Out."

Seemingly unperturbed, she slowly rose from the bed, making sure her body was completely exposed to him. His anger boiled hotter and he tore the sheet from the bed and threw it at her. "I thought you might wish to help me. I am so lonely and sad. My sister is gone and so is my friend, Jaffar. I have no one."

Now she was attempting to manipulate his sympathies. "I love my wife and I would never betray her trust. Never! Now, get up, get dressed and get out." He stormed from the room.

"I just needed a bit of comfort. Is that so much to ask?" she called after him.

He grabbed his shirt and slammed out of the room, fastening his clothes as he ran up to the deck. He spotted Olivia immediately. Her hands were gripping the rail so tightly, her knuckles were white. He raced to her, but she did not spare him even a glance. Tears coursed down her cheek and dripped onto the wood she held. She had seen Amelia in his bed and him unclothed, but she must not have seen his anger at the other woman or his complete rejection of her.

"It was not what you think," he choked out, sickened that she should be so hurt.

She didn't look at him or answer. She just stared out to sea.

"I thought it was you in the bed. I swear it," he stammered.

Olivia very slowly turned her head and glared at him. "Because we look so much alike?"

"She was under the covers. Oh, God, please believe me," he pleaded. "I would never touch her. I would never touch any woman but you." Terror that he might lose her over this constricted his chest.

191

"Go away, Tristan. Go back and finish what you were doing," The words tumbled out coldly.

"I wasn't doing anything. I swear to you." He reached for her shoulder, but she pulled away as if burned.

"Do not touch me," she ground out. "Ever again."

"You don't mean that. She did this on purpose. You have been naught but good to her." His voice had risen with his anger. "This was by her wicked designs. I beg you, do not fall into her trap." He reached out a hand and inched closer and this time Olivia didn't move away. There must have been something in his tone or his words, because she finally turned to look at him.

"Tell me what happened," she whispered.

"I saw someone in the bed. I assumed it was you."

"That is why you took off your clothes." There was a trace of doubt still.

"Olivia, that woman is naught to me and you know it. I love only you. But she is trying to sabotage that, and I cannot imagine why." He resisted the urge to get down on his knees. He worried it would look as if he were guilty. But, he would, by damn, if she demanded it. He would do anything to have her believe him.

"She wants you for herself."

Tristan scoffed. "Does she? Or does she want what another has?"

Olivia frowned, clearly puzzled. "Why do you ask that?"

"It just strikes me that she is the kind of woman who does what she needs to get what she wants. And now I know how wrong I was about her."

"But a short time ago, you were defending her." Olivia puckered her lips in mock ridicule.

"I was giving her the benefit of the doubt. But, after

her behavior today, I will no longer think the best of her. In fact, I will not think of her at all."

Olivia's expression softened. "It was as you say?" she whispered.

"It was, my love." He held out his arms and she moved into them. He held her ever tighter, appreciating how close he came to losing her through the odious machinations of another. "And I will spend the remainder of my days making certain I never see that pained expression on your face ever again."

***

When Olivia had opened the cabin door, her heart had stopped beating. Tristan was sleeping with Amelia, and right under her nose? Her first reaction had been shock, followed by hurt, and finally rage. When Tristan clarified what had happened, she knew in her bones he was telling the truth. She had thought him sympathetic to Amelia, as she had been at first. The she-devil had used that compassion perhaps in hopes he would leave Olivia. But she underestimated Tristan and his devotion. And, for a brief, shameful moment, Olivia had too. In fact, Olivia wondered if such a woman could even begin to understand love like that.

Once Tristan explained, and Olivia knew he spoke the truth, she recalled how Amelia had been with Jaffar. She had feigned madness and weakness as a means to manipulate. And she had gone after Olivia in Morocco, no doubt to enhance her own standings. It was no secret that anyone with valuable information for the sultan would rise in the ranks. Possibly Amelia accepted she was to remain in the harem and had decided to make the best of it. And when she saw an opportunity to escape, she opted to use that to her advantage, as well.

Even in her own naivete, Olivia was certain a woman like Amelia was never without a plan. So what was next? It was a worrisome question.

Olivia swiped a wayward strand of her hair floating on the sea breeze behind her ear and glanced back at the hatch door leading below deck. "I do not trust her."

"Nor I. We have another week or so remaining on this voyage. I suggest we all keep our distance from her," Tristan said, sagely stroking his chin.

"We must warn Leo and Felix, although I do not think she would bother with them unless she thought she could gain their loyalty."

"Why do you say she would not bother with them?" Tristan asked.

"Have you not listened to her comments? 'I am nobility'," Olivia said, mocking the other woman.

"So she believes them beneath her?" Tristan asked, his brow creasing.

Olivia nodded. "She does."

\*\*\*

No one missed Amelia when she did not appear at the evening meal. When Tristan told them what had transpired earlier, no one was surprised she chose to avoid their company.

"Maybe she'll starve," Maggie said. "It would serve her right after what she did today."

"I doubt it. I think she has been stockpiling food," Tristan remarked.

"What? Why?" asked Felix.

"The captain said supplies are missing from the kitchen," Tristan answered.

"Maybe she is clever enough to hedge her bets," Leo suggested. "If she thought she might cause offense, she could keep to her cabin for the remainder of the voyage without worrying about her supper."

"I never liked her," said Maggie. "Didn't trust her, either. Especially when I found out how she tried to get Jaffar to go to the sultan and lie about Olivia."

"Poor Jaffar," said Olivia. "I feel terrible about him. He died because he fell in love with her." A wave of sympathy swept over her.

"I thought those men, well, you know," said Leo.

"They lost their manly parts, not their souls or their hearts." Olivia responded. "And the way he looked at Amelia...he was smitten. It cost him his life."

"At least we all now know what she is like. So we can protect ourselves from her plotting." This from Maggie.

"I, for one, cannot wait to touch English soil," Tristan smiled. He held up his cup. "Let's drink a toast to that."

# Chapter Thirteen

A day passed, then two and three. Amelia had not appeared on deck or at meals and, although all were happy not to have to spend time with her, the tension still tainted the air. The captain sent a man to check on her, but she sent him away.

Olivia and Tristan concentrated on being together, as did Leo and Maggie. Felix talked about seeing his wife again. Being around the two happy couples made him appreciate what he had at home.

As they sat at supper one night, Tristan held up his cup again. "The captain said we should be sailing into the Thames by day after tomorrow. To coming home." The others cheered and joined in the toast. The stress and misery suddenly fell away. They were safe and soon they would be with their families. It was definitely cause for celebration. Just as they were beginning the meal, Amelia appeared and sat down at the table. A pall fell over the room.

"I came to apologize. Especially to you, Olivia and Tristan." She bowed her head over her raised, pressed palms. "I have no idea what got into me, but I behaved disgracefully." She kept her gaze lowered. "I don't imagine you can ever forgive me. I was just suddenly so overcome, you understand, after all I've lost. I sought a

196

moment of solace and I suppose I thought being held would ease the agony. After all I've suffered." She sniffed loudly. "But I promise I will never cause you another problem." She turned her head away, as if she was too disgraced to look at any of them.

She actually sounded sincere. She even managed a tear or two to slip down her cheeks and splash on the table. Olivia looked over at Tristan, who was frowning. Then her gaze settled on Maggie, who clearly wasn't buying this apology. Nor was Olivia. She had never seen a better performance. She had praised herself on her abilities as a mummer, but her "sickness" act was weak in comparison to this. But men could be more easily swayed by a pitiable female with tears in her eyes. It appeared this was not the case this time and Olivia was relieved.

After supper, when they were lying together, Olivia decided not to talk about Amelia and was a little disheartened when Tristan brought up the subject of the other woman.

"When we arrive home, I think it is our duty to see Amelia safely home. Do you not agree?" he asked.

Olivia stared at him in disbelief. "You do not mean we should stay with her longer than necessary?"

"Of course not. I meant I can have some of the crewmen escort her."

"Can we not discuss her more tonight? It leaves a bitter taste in my mouth," Olivia said.

"Well, how about if I replace that with a sweet kiss?"

\*\*\*

A shard of moonlight illuminated the cabin. Olivia turned over and was suddenly awake. Tristen had just put his arm around her waist. She snuggled her back against him, taking comfort in his nearness, when she felt something was amiss. She blinked to see more clearly in the shadows, but there was nothing there. She took a deep breath to dismiss her trepidation and pulled the cover up tighter when suddenly, all hell broke loose.

She was shoved back against the wall and Tristan surged from the bed. He landed squarely against a man. A very large man.

Jaffar? But he was dead.

Their bodies connected with a thud. They wrested to the floor and collided into the table and chairs. But the furniture was nailed down; it only shook without giving way.

It was all happening so fast. Grunts filled the air. A ray of moonlight caught the silvery edge of a knife. Olivia watched in horror as Jaffar slashed it back and forth, seeking to sheath it into Tristan's body. Fright coursed through her like a burning stream of fire. She danced back and forth on the cot, looking for an opening, some way to help the man she loved.

She wanted to call out, but she held the rising scream, afraid it might distract her husband. There was naught she could do. The room was so very dark and even though her eyes had adjusted, the bodies were entwined, and she could not discern who was who.

A terrible grunt rent the air and Olivia's stomach clenched. But they fought on. Jaffar was huge, but Tristan was a trained fighter.

They crashed into the cot beneath her just as the cabin door slammed open. Leo and Felix stood motionless, taking in the scene. The lantern in Leo's hand illuminated the room, and the vision before them was terrifying. Each man had his hands around the other's throat. But Jaffar was dominating. And where was the blade?

Tristan bucked, thrusting his hips upward and Jaffar was thrown to the side. Tristan was on top now, grappling for the weapon that had been flung nearby. But Jaffar was faster. He had the knife in his grasp again and slashed it about wildly. The frenetic movements nearly stopped her heart.

"Do something," she screamed to the brothers. But they didn't move. They would if they could, but there seemed no way to offer aid. The space was too small and the men fighting too furiously. Leo finally jumped forward, then grunted as the blade of the knife caught him by the ankle. He jumped backward and smashed into the corridor wall. The sound distracted Jaffar and he lost focus only for a moment. Tristan took the opportunity and grabbed Jaffar's wrist, wrenching the knife free. But Jaffar rolled on top of him and the struggle went on unabated. Until there was a wheeze and all motion stopped. Rigid, Jaffar toppled onto Tristan. For a hideous moment, no one moved.

Olivia sailed off the cot and grabbed for Tristan just as Felix rolled Jaffar to the side. The knife protruded from Jaffar's chest; his expression frozen in the rictus of death.

"Oh, God, Tristan, are you hurt?" Hysterical, she ran her hands over him and one came away sticky when she grazed his shoulder. "He stabbed you!".

She could discern his smile in the dim light. "I am fine. It is naught but a scratch." He scooted upright and peered over at Jaffar. "Is he dead?"

"Quite dead, my lord," Felix answered, leaning over the lifeless body of Jaffar.

Maggie had raced down the corridor and dropped to her knees beside Leo, who was staunching the blood flowing from his foot with his hand.

"Leo?" Tristan asked.

"I am ashamed to say the gash knocked me off balance."

"Thank goodness," Maggie whispered. She tore a strip of linen from the bed and wrapped Leo's foot.

The captain and several of his crew crowded the corridor. "What happened? Is anyone hurt?"

Tristan quickly relayed the details. "Leo, do you need a doctor?"

"Maggie has bandaged the wound. But thank you."

"So you clearly have this under control," the captain said.

"Captain, can you send someone to Amelia's room and see she is locked in. We will turn her over to the magistrate when we dock."

"Of course. That should be any time now. It's almost dawn," the captain said, striding into the corridor.

Tristan peered at Jaffar. "Well, that was unexpected," he announced and everyone half-laughed, half-sighed in relief.

"How is this possible?" Leo asked. "I thought he fell overboard."

"So we all thought. But it would explain the missing food." Tristan inhaled, then shook his head. "Obviously, Amelia had him secreted still in the cargo hold, just waiting for an opportunity."

"But why would he wish to kill you?" Felix asked. "What could he gain?"

"The blade was not poised over my heart. It was directed at Olivia."

Olivia recoiled at the revelation. She was the intended target. She could have been murdered…in her sleep. Her heart stuttered knowing how close she had come to death. Tremors shook her and she wrapped her arms about her waist.

Tristan reached over to cup her cheek. Fear and relief warred in his gaze. "Thank heavens I woke when I did."

"You saved me," she whispered.

He grinned. "Finally."

"It makes sense. Jaffar must have told her you were the ambassador. She wanted you, so she decided to rid herself of your wife. And Jaffar was kept as her secret weapon."

All eyes went to the man lying dead on the floor.

"I actually feel sorry for him," Olivia said. "He was truly a fool for love. And he paid for it with his life. What a wicked, duplicitous woman."

"So, what are we going to do with the bitch," Maggie sneered, barely controlling her anger. "She has done so much damage."

Maggie continued to fuss over her husband. "Can you stand?"

"I can walk," he replied, dropping his chin, clearly still a bit embarrassed by his wound and lack of aid to Tristan.

The captain was back in a trice. "She is gone. I enlisted the crew to search the ship."

"I will help you," Tristan offered.

Olivia gently pushed him back onto the bed. "You will go nowhere until I see to your wound."

A thorough inspection assured her it was only a slight cut, but she carefully washed it and covered it with a towel. As she did, tears coursed down her cheeks and she kissed the spot over and over.

"I am fine," Tristan kept assuring her.

"I know," she sobbed.

"Then why are you crying?"

"I am crying for what could have happened."

He, too, looked as if tears might slip from his eyes. "We are both safe now."

"Will you finally admit to being my rescuer and my hero?" she asked.

"I suppose," he said, his smile wider now.

*** 

Amelia's room was abandoned, and she was nowhere on the ship. They searched the cargo hold and found evidence that Jaffar had indeed been living there throughout the voyage. It was clear to everyone Amelia had asked Jaffar to do away with Olivia. If it hadn't been for Tristan's quick reactions, he might have succeeded.

"If she had succeeded in her plot, and Olivia was killed, Amelia no doubt believed she could claim Tristan for herself," Maggie speculated.

Tristan gazed at Olivia, the love shining in his eyes. "I could never love another," he said, and a flush of pleasure ran through Olivia, warming her soul.

Tristan was up on deck talking with the captain when one of the crew approached. "A small boat is missing. As is one of the crewmen."

"How close are we to the Thames?" Tristan asked the man.

"Close enough that it would be possible for that boat to make it safely to shore," the man responded.

"She must have managed to get one of my men to help her. A woman would not be able to manage alone." The captain eyes narrowed and his lips were in a thin line.

"And so she has fled," Leo snarled.

Was there no end to Amelia's depravity? Olivia wondered, disgust turning her stomach.

A more thorough search of the cabin Amelia had occupied revealed a large velvet bag tucked under the mattress. Olivia held it up. "What do you suppose this contained?"

Tristan took the sack from her. "Treasure," he answered, shaking his head. "Tazim's treasure."

"What? How is that possible?" Olivia asked.

"I don't know. I took the cache to the sultan in three such pouches. A small man took it to do an accounting."

It suddenly dawned on her. "There are no secrets in the palace."

"Jaffar would have known about the returned treasure." Maggie added.

"Jaffar must have stolen it for her," Olivia speculated.

Tristan exhaled in revulsion. "Was there anything the man would not do for her?"

"So that is how she was able to purchase such an expensive gown in Portugal. And if she has the remainder of it, she will be a very rich woman." Olivia rolled her eyes. "And to think I actually felt sorry for her."

"There will be no stopping her now," Maggie said, her arms akimbo.

"All of Tazim's wealth, gone forever," Olivia moaned. "And to her.

"Not all. I set some aside before I returned the remainder to Moulay." Self-satisfaction gleamed in his eyes and Olivia threw her arms around his neck and kissed him soundly on the mouth.

"You are a clever and brave man."

"It makes me sick to think that woman got away with

so much, Maggie gritted out, "including the coin and jewels that belonged to another.".

"I suppose it is no worse than returning it to Moulay," Tristan said sadly.

"I think we should go after her," Leo said, his stance rigid. "What was her surname? Do you know?" This was directed at Olivia.

"Caswell. She said her father was a viscount. It cannot be so difficult to find them." She looked to Tristan. "Leo is right. She cannot be allowed to get away with this."

"Then it is settled," Tristan agreed. "Let us make port and assure our families we are safe and well. Then Leo, Felix, and I should seek out Amelia's family."

"I think you forgot someone," Olivia piped up.

"Someones," Maggie added, sidling up close to Olivia.

"We are going with you." Olivia declared. Maggie nodded.

"Have you not had enough adventure for one lifetime?" Tristan asked.

"We are in this together," Olivia huffed. "All or none."

"Yes," Maggie agreed. "All or none."

\*\*\*

Tristan and Olivia returned to his cabin. In the light of day, they could clearly see the destruction from the fight the night before. Jaffar had been buried at sea, but some of his blood still stained the wooden slats on the floor.

Bedding was scattered and part of a chair was broken.

A few books littered the corners and papers were flung about.

Olivia gathered the blankets and returned them to the cot. She turned to Tristan kneeling and prying up part of the floor. She wondered what the devil he was doing. A panel came away and he stuck his hand into the opening. When he pulled it back, jewels dripped between his finger.

Olivia fell to her knees next to him, examining the cache. She smiled. "Tazim will be pleased."

"Oh, I don't think he cares about this. He will be pleased you are safe."

"All the same, he cannot be unhappy to have some of it back." Olivia bit her lower lip. "Do you think we can recover the rest?"

"We can try."

# Chapter Fourteen

Leo, Maggie, and Felix hired a carriage at the port. The plan was to go to their home, visit with their family and, after a few days, return to Kincaid Manor. They would form a plan and then seek out Amelia Caswell. Olivia had no idea what they would say to Amelia's family. She could only imagine they would not be well received. But, they had no choice.

Meanwhile, Tristan and Olivia would go to her family and stay until the others re-joined them. Olivia asked that they ride home, so Tristan acquired two horses.

"It is getting late," he said. "Do you wish to stop at an inn for the night and get some rest?"

"No. I am quite anxious to be home. If we hurry, we can make it in time for the evening meal." She was quivering with anticipation.

Dusk softened the sky with shades of pink, orange, and blue when Kincaid Manor finally came into view. They kicked their horses into a gallop. A groomsman, a puzzled look on his face, ran out to meet them. Once he saw Olivia, his face split with a grin. "Lady Olivia. Lady Olivia," he cried.

She put a finger to her lips to quiet him. "I wish it to be a surprise."

"Yes, my lady. Sorry, my lady." He dropped his chin.

206

She patted his shoulder. "Do not apologize for giving me such a warm and lovely welcome."

His blush was visible even in the fading light. He took the reins and led their horses away. Olivia then raced to the front door and eased it open. She could tell the family was in the dining room and slipped inside the front hall. Tristan was right behind her as she tiptoed into the room. For a moment, no one noticed them standing in the entryway.

"We are very hungry. Could you set another two places, perhaps?" she asked, as though she had just come down the stairs for the meal.

Lady Philippa let out a cry of joy and jumped from her seat. Olivia was wrapped in her arms so tightly she was finding it difficult to draw breath. And she was nearly crushed on all sides as Catherine and Shera joined Philippa. It was hard to contain her giggles and tears of happiness.

After a moment, the women stepped back to examine her. "You are back! You are back!" Tears of joy wet Catherine's cheeks.

"Are you hurt. Did they hurt you?' Philippa turned Olivia back and forth, then spun her back and hugged her again.

"Thank the Lord." Shera closed her eyes in what seemed a silent prayer of thanks.

The men surrounded her now, as well, all talking at once. She embraced and kissed each of them in turn. "I will tell you everything. But we are starving."

John greeted Tristan, who was still hovering in the doorway, with a pat on the back. "You kept your word. Thank you. Thank you."

Then the earl stepped up, quickly swiping at the

moisture in his eyes. "There are no words," he said quietly.

"Thank you," Tazim echoed.

Two more places were set at the table and Tristan and Olivia took their seats. In between bites and swallows of wine, they recounted their adventures. Their audience alternately cried out, clapped their hands, and shook their heads in sympathy.

"You have brought her home as you promised," the earl announced when they had completed their recounting. "Tristan, there is no reward great enough."

"We are finally free of that terrible place," Olivia said. "They think we are all dead from the plague that I carried or, at the very least, I have tainted everyone I touched."

"That is true," Tazim agreed. "The sultan fears nothing more than disease. Even if he thinks you survived, he will have no desire to associate with those who might bring sickness."

"What a clever plan. Who came up with it?" the earl inquired.

"Did I not mention that part?" Olivia asked. "It was Bekir's twin brother."

"Bekir has a twin?" Philippa asked, her head angled in question.

"Yes," John responded. "His name is Braheem." He turned to Olivia. "Did he not wish to come with you and escape?" His eyebrows drew together.

She smiled. "He desired to remain and help any and all he could. I am quite certain he is now the head eunuch in the harem. But he wanted me to let Bekir know he is well and happy."

"We will make certain he is told," Shera said.

The family then recounted all that had happened the

night Olivia was taken, describing the harrowing details of how Catherine was lured to the old ruin and how little Malcolm, John and Shera's son, was held hostage. And while Nabil and some of his cohorts were overcome and killed, they had no idea others had been instructed to take Olivia, too."

Obviously, Nabil wanted revenge. Olivia wondered what might have happened differently if Nabil had seen his full plan to fruition. She gave thanks to heaven he had failed.

"Tristan had come up with the idea to be an ambassador and went to Morocco," John added.

Tristan dropped his head, embarrassed at the praise that followed. "My reward is Olivia's safe return home." Olivia found his embarrassment endearing.

"Speaking of rewards...Tristan, is it still your wish to marry my daughter?" the earl inquired. He took a step forward to Tristan, his palms up.

"I think the family will definitely approve of a match between you two," John said, looking to the earl for assent. The earl nodded and Olivia was overjoyed. Her family's approval meant everything to her.

Tristan blew out a breath. "That is indeed happy news. Since..." He turned his gaze to Olivia, who was worried they all might be disappointed to learn they were already married.

"...since we are already married. We handfasted once we were away from the clutches of Moulay," Olivia finished for her husband.

Lady Philippa frowned. "Handfasted? But that is an ancient custom. Is it even valid?"

The earl nodded. "It is quite legal, my dear. Especially if there were witnesses."

"There were," Tristan affirmed. "The Roberts brothers were witnesses."

"Well, that is not acceptable," Philippa declared.

Panic seized Olivia by the throat. Would her mother truly object to the union?

"My youngest daughter is to have a proper wedding celebration and I intend to see to it." Philippa said, smiling.

Olivia laughed, relieved and delighted at the prospect. She turned to Tristan, who was beaming. They would have their full celebration after all.

"A welcome home party and a wedding!" Catherine clapped her hands.

"Oh," Tristan said. "There is one more thing." He reached into his shirt and withdrew a small purse, which he handed to Tazim. "A gift from the sultan." Olivia could barely contain her pleasure at watching this.

Tazim opened the pouch and his eyebrows shot up. "What is this? And how…?"

Tristan shrugged. "When I turned over the treasure to Moulay, I held back some. I thought it only fair."

"Then you are entitled to keep this." Tazim attempted to hand it back.

"No, we both want you to have it." Olivia placed her hands on Tazim's. "You were willing to give it up for me. You should have it back."

Tazim shook his head and smiled. "Thank you."

"I must say there is a task I must see to before this matter is done," Tristan announced solemnly.

All eyes went to him. "After the party, I intend to seek out the Caswell's. As we told you, Amelia not only tried to have Olivia killed, she also has the remainder of Tazim's treasure. I need to find her and see that justice is served."

210

Olivia knew how wily Amelia could be. And wondered at the outcome. She was certain it would not be easy.

"Then I will go with you," John declared.

"As will I," Tazim echoed.

"My men will be joining me, the ones who accompanied me. I think five men might be more than is necessary. We should be able to find and subdue one woman," Tristan stated.

John and Tazim agreed, though they were clearly disappointed.

"And I am joining you," Olivia declared.

"You will do no such thing, my girl," the earl avowed, placing his hand on his daughter's shoulders. "Now that you're home and safe, I am determined you are never to be put at risk again."

Before she could protest, her father held up his palm in dismissal. "There will be no discussion."

She knew there would be no way to convince her father otherwise. She desperately wanted to see Amelia brought to justice, but she would have to allow the men to see to it.

\*\*\*

No one could plan and execute a party more efficiently than Lady Philippa. In three days' time, she had arranged for the priest, musicians, and the kitchen to prepare a feast. Olivia was fitted for a new gown, blue, just as she had imagined. And Tristan was treated like royalty. He had saved Olivia and nothing was too good for him now.

The family recognized the handfasting, so the couple

was not separated during the preparations. It made everyone feel better that Olivia was never left alone, which suited her. She could not have asked for a better companion than her husband.

People began to arrive, and the wedding was to take place at the end of the week. Leo, Felix and Maggie joined them, and Maggie was fluttering with excitement.

"Leo's family is so kind. So welcoming. They, too, celebrated our nuptials, but it was not as grand as your fete will be." There was no envy in her tone. She was delighted for Olivia and Tristan.

"Ah, but you shall share in the festivities. You, too, are newly wed and we saved each other from the terrible fate that would have destroyed us all." Olivia hugged her friend, her joy filling her with light.

The day finally came. The main hall was filled with long feasting tables, roses and wildflowers in the centers. Another table groaned with all manner of delicious dishes, the aromas filling the air. Maggie stood with Olivia, while both Leo and Felix were with Tristan. The vows were exchanged, outside, under a tree, beneath an arbor festooned with flowering vines. Tristan slipped a magnificent ruby and diamond ring upon Olivia's finger. She looked up at him in surprise.

"It was my grandmother's. I sent for it." There was such love in his gaze, Olivia was warmed to her toes.

There was only one more thing to complete her special day. Olivia asked the priest to bless Leo and Maggie as well. Tears welled in Maggie's eyes and she whispered 'thank you' after the priest finished. Leo, too, gave his thanks in a single nod.

In the receiving line after the ceremony, Tristan's mother, Lady Ella, was one of the welcomed guests. She knew he had been traveling, but she had no idea of the actual mission. Later, after she had time to enjoy the festivities, her son enlightened her and her knees went so weak, she had to be helped to a chair. Olivia was instantly at her side.

"Your son is such a brave and wonderful man," Olivia gushed. "You should be so proud."

Lady Philippa joined them. "He saved my daughter. Without him, she would have…well, I cannot even entertain what might have happened."

"His father would be very proud." She raised her gaze to Philippa. "My first husband died young and I cannot say I missed him. He was a cruel man. And Peter, my eldest, I fear took after his father. But then I met Tristan's father. He was the love of my life. Unfortunately, he, too, was taken from me—thrown from a horse and broke his neck." She pressed her lips together at the painful memory. "But I have Tristan and he is my comfort." She gazed up at her son, who smiled at her.

"If I had known where you were going, I don't know how I would have survived the worry," Lady Ella whispered.

"Which is why I did not feel the need to tell you," he grinned.

She grabbed his hand. "Have you finished with adventures?" she asked, her tone pleading.

"Almost," he teased.

And then the party began in earnest. Wine flowed, food was consumed, the musicians played and everyone danced the night away. After so much misery, everyone was light-hearted and joyous. Olivia had the time of her life—twirling, eating, drinking and laughing with family and friends. And stealing kisses with her soulmate.

As dawn broke and the sky was decorated with the golden purples and blues of the day, the exhausted guests sought their rest. Olivia and Tristan curled up together after making love.

"We will leave in two days," Tristan whispered. "But I promise, I will come back to you as soon as possible. I never want to be away from you ever again."

"Then let me go with you." She dreaded being apart from him, especially since she knew he might face danger.

"No. I have no idea what we might encounter, and you will be safe here. If you accompanied us, I would do naught but worry about you. And besides, I dare not go against my new father-in-law's wishes."

"What do you think you will find?" A tremor crawled up her spine at the thought of Amelia. Who could imagine what machinations the woman might invent? She had proven herself ruthless and would do whatever it took to save herself.

"I know not. Her family may wish to protect her, in which case we will have to assert our rights in this."

"I do not like the sound of that." Olivia bit her lower lip.

"We will be fine. And we will see done what is right. Now go to sleep or I will be forced to make love to you again."

"But," she grinned, "I am not tired."

***

Tristan actually ached at the thought of leaving Olivia. He and the others mounted and prepared for their journey, and all he could think was how much he would miss her.

"How far is their estate?" Olivia asked.

"Two days' ride. We should be back by the end of next week, at the latest." He tried to reassure her as well as himself. "I will miss you."

"And I you," she replied, placing a kiss on her finger and touching his thigh.

They said their goodbyes and all who remained watched as the horses cantered away. It had been decided Maggie would stay at Kincaid Manor until Leo returned. As much as his family made her welcome, Olivia thought Maggie would be more comfortable here. Olivia assured them they would find things to occupy themselves until they returned, although it would be a painful separation.

The ride northeast was uneventful. John knew the location of the Caswell holdings and, based on the map he had drawn for them, it was not difficult to locate the estate. On the afternoon of the second day, the manor house appeared in front of them. It was a residence well kept, surrounded by lush gardens and rolling countryside.

As the men approached, they noticed there was no one in evidence. Unchallenged, they trotted to the front entry and dismounted. Two grooms appeared and took their horses without question as to their business. Tristan girded himself for an unwelcome reception and possible strife. He also needed to control his desire to strike the woman who had threatened Olivia.

The three walked to the door and knocked.

An older woman with grey hair tucked under a cap and wearing an apron answered.

"Yes?"

"We would like an audience with the viscount," Tristan announced.

"He is not at home." The woman licked her lips and gazed at them with disinterest.

"Do you know when he will return? We have urgent business," Tristan continued.

The old woman gave them a wan smile. "There is no business so urgent the viscount would bother with," she replied.

Tristan frowned and glanced at the brothers, who both shrugged their confusion. Tristan stepped up. "How about the viscountess? Is she in residence?"

The maid nodded. "She is, but she is not receiving visitors."

"She will want to see us," Tristan said. "We are here about her daughters."

The woman paled and gasped. "What about them?"

"We would really prefer to discuss this with the viscountess," Tristan said.

"You must know she is still in mourning since they were found." The old woman glared at the men. "What could you tell her she doesn't already know? She has grieved enough."

This made no sense. The daughters were *found*? "Just a few moments of her time. Perhaps we have some answers." He was politely insistent.

The maid brightened. "You know more about who killed them?"

*Killed them*? But only Charlotte was dead, unless Amelia had been recently killed. He looked again to the brothers, but they were as baffled as he.

The old woman shuffled her feet, but ultimately ushered them into the foyer and led them to a sitting room. "Wait here. But I beg you, do not upset her. Lady Eleanor has suffered enough of late."

Tristan wondered how they could tell the woman about her daughter and ask as to her whereabouts without upsetting her.

216

"Something is very odd here," Leo said once the old woman left the room.

"I agree. None of it makes sense," Tristan concurred. He was definitely suspicious and he had a bad feeling about all this.

Moments later, a small woman with dark brown hair and dressed in black, walked in slowly, as if the action pained her. Her lack of wrinkles suggested she couldn't be past her fourth decade, but her shuffling movements were those of a woman much older. She peered at the men, but did not seem alarmed. Just very sad.

"I am Lady Eleanor. Are you from the magistrate?" she asked, as if dreading the response.

"No, my lady. We have come about your daughter, Amelia," Tristan said.

"God rest her soul." A tear slipped down the woman's pale cheek.

"When did she pass?" Felix asked, clearly thoroughly confused.

"Why it's been…" the woman choked on a sob. She composed herself, then spoke again. "Three months now. Both of them."

Leo spoke up. "Forgive me, my lady, but we are very confused. Lord Tristan here was in Morocco with them." He motioned between him and Felix. "As were my brother and I."

The woman frowned, glaring at them. "Do you dare jest with me at such a time. I am mourning my daughters." Her voice was ragged.

Tristan knelt on one knee in front of her to show respect and sympathy. "Forgive me, Lady Eleanor. There must be some confusion. Let me explain."

Eleanor narrowed her eyes. "Go on," she urged, clearly containing her anger.

"My wife was kidnapped and taken to Morocco. On the ship with her were two women who introduced themselves as the Caswell sisters."

Eleanor stepped back and sank into a chair. Her nostrils flared. "Can you describe these women?"

The men exchanged glances, not understanding what was transpiring. That uneasy feeling in Tristan's gut was growing.

"They were small, with pale skin and blonde hair," Tristan answered.

Eleanor closed her eyes, pain etching across her forehead. She put her hand to her heart and lifted her gaze. "What happened to them?" she whispered.

"I'm afraid Charlotte was killed by the Moroccan sultan, but Amelia survived and escaped," Tristan explained.

"Of course she did." Eleanor sat back in the seat. "And where is *Amelia* now?" Her face was tight with vexation.

"We were trusting you would tell us," Leo said.

Eleanor nodded. "I thought that was the case. That there was some sinister plot. My husband didn't believe me. He said it wasn't possible. But then, he always thinks the best of people."

No one spoke, hoping she would elaborate. Finally, she went on.

"My daughters, Charlotte and Amelia, were killed some months ago. They were found in the lake behind the manor. The magistrate determined they had been drowned." She heaved a sigh, barely controlling her misery. "I suppose it was thought they would never be discovered. But they floated to shore." Now her tears came in earnest.

218

"I don't understand. They were on the ship with Olivia," Tristan declared. "I saw them in Morocco."

Eleanor raised her teary gaze to his. "You must have seen their ladies' maids."

"What?" All the men said in unison. The implication hit Tristan with the force of a runaway horse.

"Are you saying their maids did away with them and took their places?" Tristan asked, his disbelief obvious. How was it possible to be so heartless, so self-serving? What these women had done was unspeakable. "How did the women come to be here?"

Eleanor swallowed. "Several years ago, it became apparent our daughters needed help with dressing and their coiffures. They had outgrown their nanny and it was time to get them some maids of their own. One day, these sisters appeared at our door. The younger one, she always seemed to be the most vocal, announced they had heard we were looking to employ some servants. Of course, I had mentioned the need to some of our friends, so I didn't doubt their veracity. And the women seemed perfect, so well-spoken and knowledgeable as to the ways of polite society."

"So you hired them and invited them into your home?" Tristan said this more in understanding than in judgment.

"Something I will regret to the last day I live." Eleanor closed her eyes for a moment. Then she inhaled and continued.

"The viscount and I left to go on a short sojourn. When we returned three days later, the girls and their maids were gone. They had told the housekeeper they were going to the marketplace and no one questioned them. But they never returned. Days passed and we heard nothing. That is, until the magistrate appeared with the terrible news." Now, she broke down into more sobbing.

Tristan stepped outside the room and called for a servant to bring Eleanor some brandy. A maid appeared with a glass a moment later and Eleanor gratefully sipped, then coughed, but regained her composure.

"It was then we realized jewelry and gowns were missing." This last was said with a terrible finality.

Tristan shook his head. "I am so sorry. But to be clear, you are saying that the maids killed your daughters and took their place." These revelations were stunning. How unfathomable to have your children murdered by people you took into your home out of charity. How devastating it must be for her to wake up every morning without her children.

"Yes," Eleanor replied, her color rising with her anger. "That is exactly what I'm saying. But how they found themselves on a ship to Morocco is beyond me."

"I have no doubt they were actually kidnapped," Leo answered.

"So the one you know as Amelia is still at large?" she asked. There was no pity in her voice.

Tristan nodded. "She escaped onto our ship with a male companion when we were sent from Morocco. But she managed to take valuables that do not belong to her. We think the man with her stole for her."

"And what of this man? Are they still together?" Her eyebrows raised in question.

"I killed him," Tristan said flatly. "He tried to attack my wife and now I have no doubt it was at the behest of Amelia."

"Would you mind not calling her by that name? That is, was, my daughter's name, not hers. Her name is Claire. Her sister was Flora." A tear slipped down her cheek.

"I am so sorry," He waited a moment, then continued. "So you have no idea where she might have gone?"

"She wouldn't dare return here. But then again, it is a big country, is it not?" Eleanor said this with heavy sadness.

"I cannot imagine she would take the chance to use your name again. Which means she will be that much more difficult to trace," Tristan said, angrily. "But I will not rest until she is found and punished for her misdeeds."

"I hope you find her and she gets what she deserves." The woman narrowed her eyes, her hate for this woman clearly reflected in their depths.

It was time to depart. Tristan, along with the brothers, thanked Lady Caswell, bade her good-bye, and set off toward home.

"Where do you think she would go?" Felix inquired.

"If she has the treasure, she is a very wealthy woman now. She might purchase an estate or travel to another country. There is no telling," Tristan said with frustration. "I have no doubt she and her sister killed the Caswell girls and she manipulated Jaffar. Someone so ruthless will be difficult to find."

"So you intend to let it go?" Leo asked.

"Oh, by no means. I stand by what I said to Lady Eleanor. I will never rest until this Claire is found and punished."

# Chapter Fifteen

It had been a pleasant few days for Olivia, although she missed Tristan and was anxious for his return. Maggie was excellent company and her family accepted her instantly.

Soon, life returned to normal and the memory of the terrible things that had transpired began to fade.

One night at dinner, while they were happily talking and enjoying that they were together, Tazim clinked his wineglass with his fork. All eyes turned to him.

"We have an announcement to make," he said, his smile wide.

Catherine's cheeks pinked and she, too, grinned.

Olivia clapped her hands in delight. "You're having a babe!"

Tazim frowned. "How could you possibly know that?"

Shera and Olivia both laughed.

"It is hard to miss the sound of retching every morn," Shera stated, nodding. "We were wondering when you were going to tell us."

Catherine pressed her hand to her lips. Then she turned to Shera. "Will the sickness ever stop?"

"Eventually."

"Well, that's encouraging," Catherine replied.

"It's worth it," Shera said.

"I know. We can't wait." Catherine gazed at Tazim as if he was the only man in the world.

The men gathered round for congratulatory pats on Tazim's back, while the women kissed Catherine on the cheek. Olivia was thrilled for them. And she was looking forward to the day when she, too, could have one or two of her own and Tristan's. Then they all resumed partaking of the meal.

"I think it might be time to consider hiring some help. Two toddlers and a newborn will be quite the handful," Philippa suggested.

"I think that is a grand idea," added the earl.

"I shall put out the word among my friends tomorrow. Certainly they can recommend some reliable women who love children." Philippa's eyes were shining with joy. She pressed her palms against her heart. "I am the luckiest of women."

\*\*\*

It had been nearly a week and Tristan should return any day. Anticipation made Olivia's blood quicken. She found she did not sleep well if he was not beside her. Nightmares plagued her, visions of the harem and people being chased and crying out for help. She would wake up crying and knew she must work to rid herself of these demons. The misery was in the past, she would concentrate on the wonderful things in her life.

She thought she might to take a bath to relax. The tub was brought, and the hot water poured. She added scented oil and was gathering towels when she heard the door open and close softly. Thinking it was her maid, Jane, she didn't turn, about to disrobe.

223

"Hello, Olivia."

The sound of that voice froze her heart. She spun around and faced the hated visage.

"Did you miss me?" Amelia grinned like the demon she was.

Olivia forced herself to remain calm. "How did you get in here?" Perhaps if she could keep Amelia talking, she could think of a way to overpower her.

Amelia cackled. "Why, I am the new nanny. Your mother hired me this morning and thought it might be a grand idea if I acquainted myself with the family before the new baby comes."

With her mother asking around about a hiring someone to help, Amelia must have found out and manipulated her way in. And, Olivia knew as well as anyone that Amelia could manipulate.

"What do you want?" Olivia asked. "You certainly don't need money, since we know you had Jaffar steal the treasure for you."

"So, you figured that out, did you?" Amelia had begun pacing, effectively blocking the door. "Poor Jaffar. No giblets and so in love. Did he really believe I would settle for half a man?"

"What do you want, Amelia?" Olivia repeated.

"Actually, my name is Claire. I worked for those little bitches before Flora and I took care of the Caswell sisters." Her tone was malicious, suggesting they had permanently done away with the other girls.

Realization crashed in on her and it was almost too horrible to contemplate. "You and your sister…"

"Flora was not my sister," Claire sneered. "We were just similar enough in appearance. Too bad they killed her. She had her uses. But I, of course, was the smart one."

"Not so smart you didn't manage to get kidnapped." *Keep her talking.* Olivia frantically searched the room. She needed an advantage. Her blood thrummed in her veins. This was not Morocco. There were no guards. There had to be a way.

"Yes, we did get kidnapped, but that worked to my advantage, now didn't it. Of course, you know what I look like. You and that miserable *husband* of yours. But, if I do away with you, he will not care what happens to him. That will make him very vulnerable. Then, with both of you gone, I will be free to go on with my new identity. I may even be you." She bared her teeth in a sick smile.

"People know me. You cannot maintain a charade like that." Catherine defeated Nabil with a hairpin. There had to be something she could use. It helped the woman was not in her right mind.

"And are you so well known in France?" Claire taunted. "I think not. The Caswell's weren't." Her smile was demonic.

It suddenly occurred to Olivia she was still holding a vial of oil in her hand. *I just need to get close enough.*

With her thumb, she popped the seal from the top of the vial. It slipped from her grasp but landed soundlessly on the rug. Olivia took a breath and then moved a step closer to her adversary. Claire didn't seem to notice or care.

"Perhaps you're right. What could I offer you to simply go away?" Olivia closed the gap yet another inch forward.

Claire cackled again. "I have the treasure and I will be able to use the Kincaid name. I seem to step up in the peerage with each new masquerade."

Olivia burned to wipe the smile off the other

woman's face. Instead, she eased one more inch. *Close enough.* She flung the vial's contents into Claire's face. The other woman blanched, cried out, and scratched at her eyes. She lunged for Olivia, but Olivia was expecting it and moved quicker. Claire skidded on the spilled oil and lost her footing. She fell hard on her backside and Olivia was on her in a trice. Olivia reared back, made a fist, and punched Claire in the face with all her might. Claire yelped, so Olivia swung again, hitting even harder this time. Claire's head whipped back and her jaw slackened, then she crumbled back, her head smacking the floor.

Olivia was deciding if she should hit her once more to be certain she was not awake, or simply find something to bind her. Before she could decide, the door was flung open and Tristan raced into the room. He quickly took in the scene, raced to Olivia and helped her up.

"Are you all right?" He was breathless and his hands shook.

"Did you know?" she asked.

"I just arrived and you mother mentioned she had hired a new servant. Something told me to be suspicious after I met with the real Amelia's mother." He barked a laugh. "But, apparently, you had the situation well under control." He pulled her to him and kissed the top of her head.

\*\*\*

The magistrate was called and Claire was hauled away. Catherine had just finished putting soothing lotion on Olivia's sore knuckles and the family reunited in the sitting room.

"No one tells you how much it hurts to punch

someone," Olivia complained. "Although I would do it again in a second."

"If I were you, I would never make her angry," Tazim cautioned Tristan, who laughed.

"Worry not. I am planning on devoting my life to seeing to her happiness."

Tazim looked over at his wife. "All the Kincaid women are forces to be reckoned with," he said with pride.

Just then, John entered the room, grinning and holding up a knapsack. "Guess what I discovered in the woman's things."

He threw the bag to Tazim, who deftly caught it, and looked inside. His bellow of laughter echoed in the room.

"What is it?" Catherine asked.

"Well, you do not ever have to worry about starving," he responded. He held up two velvet pouches. Opening one, he pulled out a cache of jewels.

Olivia gasped. "The sultan's treasure?"

John shook his head. "Unbelievable."

"And so it is back where it belongs," the earl said. "As are we all."

# The End

# About The Author

Leslie Hachtel was born in Ohio, raised in New York and has been a gypsy most of her adult life. Her various jobs, including licensed veterinary technician, caterer, horseback riding instructor for the disabled and advertising media buyer have given her a wealth of experiences.

However, it has been writing that has consistently been her passion.

She is a bestselling author who has written twelve romance novels, including nine historicals and three romantic suspense. She also sold an episode of a TV show, and had a screenplay optioned. Leslie lives in Florida with a fabulously supportive engineer husband and her new writing buddy, Annie, a terrier.

www.ingramcontent.com/pod-product-compliance
Lightning Source LLC
Chambersburg PA
CBHW051430170626
46809CB00006B/2407